THE KILLING OF NED CHRISTIE

Cherokee Outlaw

NED CHRISTIE
by Robert J. Conley

He cooked cornbread
(mixed in the meal pounded dried squirrel)
in a huge pot:
a fire on the lid.

He was marble champion (unofficial)
of the Cherokee Nation.

They say the boys came
from miles around
to shoot for his marbles
to eat his delicious cornbread.

He was a blacksmith
a gunsmith
a legislator.

They said (the whites)
he was an outlaw.

23 men
a cannon
and dynamite
in 1892

killed him
displayed his body on a slab

posed with it
for their photograph
(something to leave their children & their children's children).

In a cemetery
where now hogs root
lie the bones of *Nede Wade.*

On the marker
now knocked down
is told

he was a blacksmith
and was
a brave
man.

From *Songs From This Earth On Turtle's Back,* edited by Joseph Bruchac, 1983, Greenfield Review Press, Greenfield Center, New York. Permission for use granted by the author.

THE KILLING OF NED CHRISTIE

Cherokee Outlaw

by Bonnie Stahlman Speer

Also by Bonnie Speer:
Errat's Garden (picture book)
Benjamin Stanley Revett: Father of Gold Dredging
Portrait of a Lawman: U.S. Deputy Marshal Heck Thomas
Moments in Oklahoma History, A Book of Trivia
Cleveland County (OK), Pride of the Promised Land
The Great Abraham Lincoln Hijack, 1876 Attempt to Steal President's Body
Hillback to Boggy
Sons of Thunder with Jess Speer
Barbie Doll Trivia Trail with Cheryl Hanlon
Miss Little Britches
Beloved Barbarian with Connie Wilson

Copyright 1990 Bonnie Stahlman Speer
First Edition Published 1990, Second Edition 2000

Library of Congress Cataloging in Publication Data:

The Killing of Ned Christie
Cherokee Outlaw

Includes endnotes, index, bibliography, iIllustrated

1. United States--History
2. Cherokee Nation
3. Outlaws

LC 99-070383
ISBN 1889683-13-2 ppr.

Published by Reliance Press
1400 Melrose Drive
Norman, Oklahoma 73069

Printed in the United States of America

To Allene J. Davis

TABLE OF CONTENTS

ILLUSTRATIONS

FOREWORD

Like so many "gunmen" living on the 19th century western frontier, Ned Christie was more than that label implies . . . and less. Other labels fit just as well— "three-quarters Cherokee," "gunsmith," "blacksmith," "marksman," "Cherokee legislator," "family man," "victim of injustice," "local hero," and "proud homeowner." One label that does not fit nearly as well is "killer," let alone such derogatory dime-novel descriptions as "blood-thirsty renegade," or "most cold-blooded fiend in the Indian Territory."

It has been said that Ned Christie killed 11 men, or even 21 men. As Bonnie Speer made perfectly clear in her 1990 book, *The Killing of Ned Christie*, the facts don't support such numbers. One time he was charged with manslaughter and found not guilty. Later he was accused of killing a U.S. deputy marshal but never stood trial. During the course of her extensive research, Bonnie came to believe that Christie died for a crime that he did not commit. Since then, the author has picked up some new stories about Christie from one of his descendants and has been able to correct a few mistakes she made a decade ago. For those reasons, but mostly because her book is out of print, this second edition is most welcome. Her conviction that Ned Christie was forced to become an outlaw because of false accusations against him remains as strong as ever . . . and nearly as strong as Christie's own conviction more than 100 years ago that he must hold out in his fortified home in the hills of the Cherokee Nation at all costs and against all odds.

Enjoy Ned Christie's *true* story.

Gregory Lalire
Editor, *Wild West* Magazine

xi

FOREWORD

Being asked to prepare a foreword for this revised edition of Bonnie Speer's book, *The Killing of Ned Christie*, is indeed an honor. Bonnie and I have shared a strong interest in Indian Territory history for many years and both of us have recognized the significance of Ned Christie in Cherokee tribal history and our nation's history.

The tragic removal of the Cherokee and other tribes from their native homelands in the East to lands west of Arkansas, remains one of the worst periods in our nation's history. Known as "The Trail of Tears," those who survived the forced march to the West preserved hope for the Cherokee's future.

Over a period of years, Cherokee leaders negotiated new treaties with the United States which basically protected the Cherokee nation's sovereignty. This included their rights to establish their own police force and judicial system. Therefore, it is no wonder that tribal political leaders, such as Ned Christie, became irate when U.S. deputy marshals, arrested Cherokee law breakers and returned them to Fort Smith. There they faced judgement before a federal judge instead of one in the Cherokee court that had been established by treaty.

Christie's outspoken bitterness about such agreements being broken by U.S. authorities soon resulted in an army of Cherokee patriots dedicated to preserving the treaty agreements made with the United States. This resulted in numerous U.S. deputy marshals being found dead in the territory and a tense situation existed, bordering on a full scale war.

Fully aware of such potential conflict, President Ulysses S. Grant ordered the Fort Smith authorities to bring in Ned Christie at all costs. Christie had been accused of murdering a U.S. deputy marshal. Christie claimed he was innocent. He had evaded the deputy marshals for five years, remaining near his fortified home east of Tahlequah, the Cherokee Nation's capital. Many individuals in the Cherokee Nation supported his cause. The explosive situation that existed required careful tactics.

After several days of selecting the best men to serve in the posse commissioned to bring down Christie and the cause he stood for, the leaders met at West Fork, Arkansas, to outfit the party for the final siege. The field cannon shipped from Ft. Scott, Kansas, to the party by rail represented the first and only time in American history that a cannon was used by the U.S. marshal service in the capture of an individual outlaw. After twenty-eight rounds from the cannon proved to be ineffective on Christie's log fort near Wauhilla, Indian Territory, and several deaths, the deputy marshals resorted to dynamite to blast the outlaw from his home. Christie, with a gun in each hand, charged from the fort towards the posse. He was brought down by some eighty rounds fired by the posse, and Ned Christie, martyr or outlaw, fell along with the cause of Cherokee Nation independence.

Often presented as one of the last Cherokee outlaws by various writers and novelists over the years, Ned Christie remains today a national hero within the Cherokee Nation. One must carefully study the issues that created the Ned Christie saga and then decide if this Cherokee patriot should be remembered as martyr or outlaw. Personally, this writer feels he was a bit of both and the lack of understanding as to what the Cherokee treaty rights fully encompassed may have caused this final tragedy.

Phillip W. Steele
Author, *The Last Cherokee Warriors*
Past Pres., National Outlaw & Lawman Association

ACKNOWLEDGMENTS

My thanks to those who have assisted me with research in this story, especially John Christie, son of Jack Christie; Mrs. John Christie; Roberta Teague, Allene J. Davis; T.L. Ballenger; Mrs. Helen Wheat, librarian, Cherokee Room, Northeastern State University, Tahlequah; the staff of the Oklahoma Historical Society; those of the Western History Collections, University of Oklahoma; Tsa-La-Gi, Cherokee Nation Museum; the staff of the National Archives; Barbara Rust, Federal Archives and Records Center, Fort Worth, Texas; Tom Clawson, National Park Service, Judge Parker's Court, Fort Smith, Arkansas, Mrs. Beatrice Maples Jones, Bentonville, Arkansas, granddaughter of Deputy Daniel Maples, Bettie Maples Halsell, his great-granddaughter; and a special thanks to eighty-six-year-old Roberta Hitchcock (at the time I interviewed her), Tahlequah, who first believed in what I was saying and put me in contact with members of the Christie family. My thanks also to Frank Parman for his support in this project and helpful criticisms and suggestions in the final polishing and to Bill Burchardt, long-time editor of *Oklahoma Today* magazine, who saw merit in my project and encouraged me. A big thanks to Phillip Steele, Springdale, Arkansas, who generously shared his material on Ned Christie from his own work on the same story. Thanks also to Roy Hamilton, a Ned Christie descendant and genealogist, who shared information from his family history, correcting some of my errors in the first edition of this book.

Bonnie Stahlman Speer
Norman, Oklahoma

INTRODUCTION

Almost one hundred years have passed since Ned Christie was shot by deputies in his log fort east of Tahlequah. Since then hundreds of articles, dime novels, short stories, poems, books, and newspaper features have been written about him, showing the fascination that he holds for writers. For the most part, however, this mass of material can be put down as unreliable.

Usually Ned Christie is portrayed as one of the most vicious killers who ever stalked the land. Typical of these tales is one collected by WPA writers in February 1938, which purported that Christie quarreled with and killed United States Deputy Marshal Dan Maples. Afterwards Christie escaped from a Bentonville, Arkansas, posse. Then, the article stated:

> In the safety of the Cherokee hills he brooded upon his act and the quarrel which preceded the killing and at length he resolved to avenge himself upon all men and especially officers. Collecting a few of his bull-blooded [sic] friends whom he could trust he organized a gang of desperadoes.
>
> Eleven murders were credited to Christie. Among his victims were two officers, an Indian woman and a half-breed boy. He was born a killer, cold blooded ruthless; no one knew when or where he would strike next. In the settlement towns, along the isolated paths to the lonely cabins of settlers he stalked relentless in his

maniacal [sic] hatred, cool in his knowledge of guns. At one time he had worked as a gunsmith, and his aim was terrifying in its accuracy.[1]

Other stories attributed as many as twenty-one killings to Christie. Invariably the writers noted the Cherokee outlaw's blood-thirsty tendencies without bothering to check the facts, for this was the blood-and-guts type of action-adventure which was filling the pages of the "dime western" then in its heyday. Most of these authors were simply rewriting the WPA story or that found in Samuel W. Harman's voluminous *Hell On The Border, He Hanged Eighty-Eight Men*, published in 1898. This book was reissued in condensed form in 1953 by Frank L. Van Eaton, and again in 1971 by the Indian Heritage Association of Muskogee as edited by Jack Gregory and Rennard Strickland.

This vast accumulation of material has generated considerable trouble for sincere writers as they try to seek out the truth about Ned Christie. Stated Robert D. Conley in his author's note in his book of western fiction *Back To Malachi*, published by Doubleday & Company in 1986:

> Some years ago while attempting research into the life of Ned Christie, I again ran across one of those references from a prominent "six-gun historian" (the phrase is Emmet Starr's) which said, in effect, that Ned Christie, a full-blood Cherokee, was the worst outlaw ever to roam the Indian Territory. That is a bold statement. I tried in vain to find evidence to substantiate that claim...[2]

Like Conley, during the course of my ten years work in gathering the material for this book, I ran into the same situation.

2

Phillip Steele attempted to publish a factual account about Ned Christie in his book *The Last Cherokee Warriors*, issued by Pelican Publishing Company in 1974. While Steele states that many sources of research were used in the preparation of the Christie portion of this book, he relies heavily on his interviews with Bill Christie, Jr., who, at the time, was an elderly patient in a nursing home and did not speak English. While Steele does add some new biographical information about Ned Christie, most of it is unsupported by documentary evidence, and numerous errors exist in his text, so it must be read with care. For instance, on page 92 Steele claims that Deputy Marshal Rusk owned a store at Oaks which Ned Christie robbed and burned. Court records show none of this to be true. Nor is Steele's statement on page 104 that court records, pertaining to the trial and sentence of Arch Wolf, have been lost. These are in the Federal Archives and Records Center, Fort Worth, Texas.

Steele makes note of the Humphrey story clearing Ned Christie of the killing of Deputy Marshal Dan Maples but attributes this information to Fred Sutton in Tulsa in 1922 instead of the *Daily Oklahoman* in 1918. Steele failed to follow through on the importance of the circumstantial evidence in the case, though he had found the information in no less reliable source than a scrapbook collected by Dan Maple's wife Maletha, which was then in the possession of Maple's granddaughter, Beatrice M. Jones, of Fayetteville, Arkansas. We are indebted to Steele, however, for the information on the Maples family which he collected in his interview with Mrs. Jones.

In contrast to the numerous stories describing Ned Christie as a cold-blooded killer, Indian writers have always regarded him as a patriot-warrior. Poets and novelists have been writing admirations and literary allusions to him since the 1920s at least. Among the

3

earliest of these fictionalized stories is that by John Oskison who was a Cherokee writer and one of the editors of the *WPA Guide to Oklahoma*. His story, *Black Jack Davey*, seems to be based in part on the Trainor father-son relationship as detailed in this book.

In Oskison's novel, the father and son want access to the land of a Cherokee named Ned Warrior, who is living with a common-law wife. Although he has been living a peaceful, non-drinking life on the farm raising his son, their accusations against Ned Warrior are based on an early crime of Ned's which has been ignored by Indian police. About half-way through the book, the posse comes in and blows up his house and shoots him down. Wounded, Ned spends some time in jail, from which he is later released. Finally he obtains his revenge on the father and son, shooting them down in a cornfield. Afterwards he reclaims his family and makes plans to settle down and live a life of peace, going into partnership, farming his land with the main character in the story. Thus Ned Warrior is a significant, but not central figure in the fiction.

In 1957 Doubleday & Company published C.H. McKennon's book, *Iron Men*. Essentially this story centers on the heroism of the deputies in Judge Issac Parker's court, and includes a detailed account of the final assault on Ned Christie from their point of view. While much of the story is based on fact, it has been fictionalized and repeats the tale found in *Hell On the Border* that Ned Christie alone was responsible for the death of Deputy Marshal Dan Maples following an accidental meeting on the creek.

It was from McKennon's book that Tulsan Ralph Powell, of Powell Productions, planned to make a movie in 1981. He contacted Will Sampson about playing the part of Ned Christie. I suggested to Powell, in Tulsa, and Sampson, with whom I spoke at a pow-wow in Norman, that they had the wrong story, and would have

4

a better tale if they would stick to the facts and tell the story from the viewpoint of Ned Christie. Powell finally put the film on hold, and then Sampson died.

The current work on library shelves by Robert J. Conley, *Back To Malachi*, was published by Doubleday & Company in 1986 under its Double D Western imprint. This book seems to be a fictionalized story of Ned Christie as seen through the eyes of one of his friends, sort of an Arch Wolf type character. In his author's note though, Conley denies that Mose Pathkiller is Ned Christie, but he admits there are similarities between the two and acknowledges that the account of Pathkiller's death is an almost direct borrowing from the Christie story.

Conley is also the author of a very good poem entitled "Ned Christie," which was printed in an anthology edited by Joseph Bruchac called *Songs From This Earth On Turtle's Back*, and is reprinted in this book.

With the vast assortment of writings to be found on Ned Christie, one might well ask why anyone should want to write another book about him. But the answer is simple: to set the record straight. When I was working on my book, *Heck Thomas, My Papa*, with Beth Thomas Meeks (Levite of Apache, 1988), something about the Ned Christie story didn't seem to ring true. I set out to discover the facts. Was Ned Christie actually guilty of the murder which started him off on the outlaw trail?

When I first began collecting material for this book in 1979, T.L. Ballenger said he didn't think I would ever be able to prove Christie's guilt or innocence one way or the other. At the time I was visiting with the ninety-six-year-old historian in his Tahlequah home.

For a while, during the course of my research, it seemed he might be right, for I found so many conflicting tales about Ned Christie. However, little by

5

little, as I began to piece the story together from various resources, what I believe to be the truth of the matter began to emerge: Ned Christie was declared guilty on circumstantial evidence, and executed for a crime he did not commit.

It was not until 1918, twenty-nine years after Christie's death, that an eyewitness to the murder of Maples shared his story with a reporter from the *Daily Oklahoman*. When I first read the story, I was delighted to find that the details were supported by other records I found in the National Archives. The reporter went on to name the real killer of Maples, and, at last, I was satisfied that the truth about Ned Christie had been revealed.

Other than Phillip Steele, most writers so far have ignored the *Daily Oklahoman* story. Why I don't know, unless they have been unaware of it. I pressed T.L. Ballenger about the matter. Did he really believe Ned Christie was guilty as he had stated in his own book, *Around Tahlequah Council Fires*, published in 1935?

"I cannot produce any evidence that Ned killed Maples except hearsay and circumstantial evidence," Ballenger admitted.

Then did Goback, Ned Christie's youngest brother and a respected member of the Rabbit Trap community, with whom Ballenger was well acquainted, really think Ned had done it?

"No," Ballenger replied. "I don't think Goback thought that. His [Ned's] picture used to hang on Goback's wall out there, and I was here talking to him one day. He pointed to Ned's picture, and he said, 'Good man. Go-o-od man!' But everything that was done in the country was laid to Ned after this marshal was killed. You couldn't tell whether Ned did it or not."

Perhaps not, but I have tried. This seems to be the first time that anyone has made use of the Fort Smith court documents to chronicle the legal records of

6

Christie and his cohorts, which gives new insights to the people and their times. What I have written, I feel, is as truthful and accurate an account as can be presented and is based on facts—verifiable evidence, carefully gathered, sifted, and evaluated—about a man, a territory, and a time.

PROLOGUE

It was a beautiful spring day, that morning of April 10, 1887, in the Cherokee Nation. It was Easter Sunday and the 140 students at the Female Seminary near Park Hill, three miles south of Tahlequah, the nation's capital, were just beginning to stir.

On the broad portico which fronted the fine old building with its graceful columns, an old man paused to enjoy the mild morning. After finishing his pipe he tapped out the tobacco embers against the northeast cornerpost, then sauntered on across the yard to his morning chores.[1]

Behind him, the hot embers smoldered in a pile of dry leaves heaped at the base of the cornerpost. A wisp of smoke soon arose. Shortly the hollow post drew the flames inside like a flue. The dry wood caught fire and an open window above the portico sucked the flames into a room where the curtains ignited. Soon an inferno was roaring. A student, smelling smoke, opened her door and found the hall ablaze. "Fire! Fire!" she shouted.[2]

Frightened half-dressed girls tumbled from their rooms. Some of the more thoughtful students threw trunks and clothing from windows of the three-story building, but most of the young ladies escaped with little more than what they had on. They huddled in fearful groups before the seminary building as the flames spread rapidly. Someone formed a fire fighting brigade with pots and pans, but the meager amounts of water had little effect on the flames.

At the first shout of fire, a young man had mounted his horse and ridden swiftly toward Tahlequah to spread the alarm. Early churchgoers heard him and responded at once.[3] Among them was Chief Dennis Bushyhead. Picking up Col. William P. Boudinot, his executive secretary, he sped in a buggy toward the scene of the conflagration. When the two men arrived, they found the walls of the building caving in. There was nothing they could do but watch the structure burn.

Soon nothing remained of the once gracious edifice but smoking ruins and the massive brick columns which had stood on three sides of the building. Bushyhead and Boudinot headed back toward town. The Cherokees took the education of their young seriously, and the loss of this school was something not be borne lightly.[4] They must rebuild at once, but first the principal chief must call the executive council into special session to deal with the matter.

Thus, in a seemingly unrelated matter, events were already set in motion which would soon bring about one of the strangest cases in American justice. Had it not been for the accidental burning of the Cherokee Female Seminary, in all likelihood, Ned Christie, a respected member of the Cherokee Legislature, would not have been in Tahlequah on May 4, 1887. The incident that occurred that night would make him one of the most hunted outlaws in the American West.

The Cherokee Female Seminary and students at Park Hill before the building burned in 1887, setting off the chain of events which sent Ned Christie on the outlaw trail. *Courtesy Western History Collections, University of Oklahoma Library.*

CHAPTER 1

The Making of the Legislator

Gold and pink rimmed the eastern horizon as smoke from the burning two-story log cabin swirled across the clearing on the hilltop. Beyond the ravine, the United States deputy marshals, stiff from their long vigil in the cold on this morning of November 4, 1892, tensed as the flames blazed higher into the sky. The roof of the building collapsed and someone shouted in warning. The next instant a tall Indian, almost hidden in the dense cloud of smoke, sped from the burning structure and headed towards the ravine. The deputies shouted for him to halt but he uttered a curse, "Damned white marshals!"[1] and ran on, his six-shooter blazing. The deputies returned his fire. Their bullets riddled his body and knocked him down. He tried to regain his feet, but another volley settled him. The cool morning breeze lifted the smoke. The deputies stepped out cautiously, unable to believe that the long chase was over, that they had finally killed the notorious Cherokee outlaw, Ned Christie.*

A legendary figure, Christie had been accused of a multitude of crimes. Chief among them was the murder of United States Deputy Marshal Dan Maples, which had set him off on his life of crime. For five years, Christie had successfully evaded capture by the federal deputies. Now they had blasted him out of his fortified

*In the Cherokee language, Christie was originally pronounced "Wattie," meaning gourd.[2]

11

log home in the Cherokee Nation east of Tahlequah and shot and killed him. Many in the crowd, which had gathered to watch the two-day battle, thought they could breathe a little easier because of this incident. Yet those who knew Christie best believed there had been a miscarriage of justice, that he had been driven into a way of life he did not want. As a member of the Executive Council of the Cherokee National Council, before turning outlaw, he was known as "a good, peaceable citizen."[3]

What brought him to this end? Was he the vicious, blood-thirsty killer some accused him of being, or had he fought only to preserve his home and freedom as others contended? The full extent of his crimes may never be known, but from a multitude of sources, much about his life can be pieced together. To fully understand his character and the events of his life, it is necessary to learn something about his background.

Born December 14, 1852, at Wauhilla, (Eagle) south of the Rabbit Trap community in the Cherokee Nation, Edward "Ned" Christie was the second child of Watt Christie and his third wife, Lydia Thrower,[4] of the bird clan. Reportedly, he had more than the usual amount of intelligence. He attended school through the third grade in the one-room schoolhouse at July Springs, a half-mile east of his father's home. Elmira Stevens, a classmate, remembered Ned as being "no different than any other child," jumping rope and laughing as he counted "one, two, three, four."[5]

Ned and his brothers, James, Jack, George, Lacy, and Goback, grew up around their father's blacksmith shop. Each became a skilled blacksmith and gunsmith. Ned in particular developed a natural appreciation for all types of weapons. By the time he was ten years old, he was reputed to be one of the best marksmen in the Cherokee Nation.[6]

---

*Named after a Cherokee schoolteacher in Georgia.

In the blacksmith shop, Ned and his brothers also became well-versed in political matters as they listened to the men of the community debate the current issues in the nation. They heard tales about the land the Cherokees had been forced to abandon in the East. Bitterness still rankled in the hearts of the elder full-bloods and was passed on to the young.

From time immemorial, the Cherokees had lived in a vast region now claimed by Tennessee, Georgia, North Carolina, and Alabama. White settlers began crowding in on all sides, demanding removal of the Indians. To protect themselves, in 1827 the Cherokees established a constitution and executive, legislative, and judicial systems similar to those of the United States. In retaliation, the Georgia legislature passed a series of outrageous laws, confiscating huge sections of Cherokee land, nullifying their laws, and forbidding them to dig for gold on their own lands.

Pressure increased on the Cherokees to remove. In 1832, a small group, who were to become known as the "Old Settlers," emigrated to Indian Territory. A minority faction signed a treaty with the United States in 1836 ceding Cherokee lands in the East for those west of the Mississippi River. During the next two years, two thousand Cherokees voluntarily joined the "Old Settlers" in Indian Territory.

At the time, according to Cherokee Evaluations of 1836, the grandfather of Ned Christie, who was also named Edward "Ned" Christie, "lived on a fine farm on the northeast side of the Hiwapee River, above the mouth of the Valley River in North Carolina." He was considered a wealthy man with a two-story, hewed log house, two hundred fruit trees, and three slaves. Ned's father, Watt Christie, then a young man of twenty-four, lived on a farm at the mouth of the Valley River. Other Christies cultivated land along the river. The enumerator of the Cherokee census noted:

This river runs into the Hiwassie River, north course, has fine seats for machinery, abounds with iron ore and had about 10,000 acres of land of very super quality. The mountain scenery here is very grand. Gold is found in abundance. I was shown by the Indians some very old looking marks of mining operations on this river, near the head of the valley. I was shown a Chalybeate spring that was out of a solid mass of bog iron ore.[7]

In later years, Watt Christie would recall how he and his brothers dug for gold, and how the remainder of the Cherokees were rounded up in 1838 by United States soldiers and herded into corrals.[8] They were forced to march westward over the "Trail of Tears." More than four thousand members of the tribe died on the infamous journey. Watt Christie and his father were among the last to go in December 1838. Records do not show whether the elder Ned Christie survived the trip but Watt Christie did and settled in Rabbit Trap.

The community lay in a broad valley in the Going Snake District, twelve miles east of Tahlequah. It was a wild and rugged area. From Flint Post Office and Dunneberg's store, the main road, which Watt Christie and his brothers helped build on a conscription basis, wound through the trees at the base of a small hill to the west. Bears roamed on Rocky Mountain to the south. Wild turkeys and deer stalked through the brush.

In the Cherokee Nation, the land was held in common, but each person could live where he wanted as long as he didn't infringe upon the rights of others. The Christies cleared most of the land in Rabbit Trap.

It took the Cherokees about twenty years to regain their former level of progress. For a short time they thought they were rid of the white man, but soon found him at the border of Indian Territory, clamoring to get in. Then had come the Civil War, and the Cherokee Nation split in its loyalties. Some of the fiercest fighting in Indian Territory occurred in the Cherokee Nation, along the Arkansas, Missouri, and Kansas borders. Bushwackers from both sides roamed the area. Refugees fled to Texas or Kansas.

Ned Christie was thirteen when the war broke out. His father, Watt Christie, refused to be driven from his land a second time. He gathered all of his family into the Wauhillau area near his home. His sons hid their hogs and cattle in the woods, and concealed objects of value. Once a band of fourteen guerrillas rode into Watt's yard. Watt and his sons hid in the barn loft where they kept shotguns loaded with buckshot. Opening fire on the guerrillas, they drove them off.[9]

Watt, forty-one, enlisted in Capt. Budd Gritts' home guards and was assigned as blacksmith to Company G of the Second Regiment of Union volunteers,[10] along with his brothers, Arch, thirty, and James, twenty.[11] Ned was left to defend the family home until the men returned. Though but a boy, with his knowledge of guns and skill in repairing and using them, in this he was perfectly capable.

Shortly after his discharge from the Union army on May 31, 1865, at Fort Gibson,[12] Watt presented Ned with a pair of .44 caliber cap and ball pistols, which the youth quickly converted into shell-percussion, five-shot pistols. He was to have many weapons during his lifetime, but these would remain his favorites and be in his hands when he died.[13]

Following the war, those who had gone away began to return to find their homes burned, fields overgrown with sassafras bushes, and hogs and cattle stolen or turned wild. Poverty ran rampant among the once prosperous Cherokees as the nation began rebuilding. The breech between the two political parties healed slowly. Many memorials and protests against railroad schemes and land grabs were presented to the National Councils The Christies were at the forefront in these bitter fights, striving to retain the rights and independence of the Cherokees.

When grown, Ned Christie established a home of his own on the west bank of Bitting Creek,* a mile north of his father's place. Dr. Bitting, a white man, operated a grist mill half-way between them. Ned cultivated a small field of corn and raised a few head of cattle and some hogs. Most of his income came from the blacksmith shop he erected next to his one-room log cabin.

Ned was always referred to as a full blood Cherokee, but his grandmother was a white woman named Betsy Christie, who died on the Trail of Tears, says Roy Hamilton. A tall, slender man with erect shoulders and a confident air, Ned's eyes were deep-set above a full, drooping mustache. He combed his dark hair neatly to one side and kept it trimmed just above his ears. He wore the simple trousers and linsey shirt of the white man with a long bandanna knotted about his neck.[15]

"Unusually handsome," like his father, Ned seemed to have his choice of Indian maidens. According to census records, he fathered three children: Mary, born to Nannie Gritts in 1873;[16] a son, James, born to his second wife, Peggie, in 1876;[17] and Jennie, born to Annie Scraper in 1881.[18] Mary and Jennie each lived with their mothers; James lived with his father. Shortly before the beginning of Ned's trouble with the deputy marshals in 1887, Peggie died and was buried in the Christie family cemetery just east of Watt Christie's home. Ned married Nancy Greece, eighteen in a traditional "joined blanket" ceremony, according to family geanologist Roy Hamilton. Nancy was a pretty, young full blood, the daughter of Ned and Arlie Greece of Rabbit Trap.[19] Census records

---

*Today this name appears on maps as Bidding Creek.

of the Going Snake District in 1890 refer to her as Nancy Christie*

It seemed natural that Ned should follow his father into politics. The Going Snake District elected him to his first term in the National Council in 1885, during the administration of Principal Chief Dennis Bushyhead, of the National Party. (Harman states Ned served in both houses of the legislature.[20]) When the National Council convened that fall, the joint body of legislators voted to place Ned on the three-man Executive Council which acted as an advisory committee to the principal chief. The position was considered an honor for only those of good moral character could be elected to this legislative body. The editor of the Cherokee Advocate noted the occasion with approval:

> Ned Christie, Daniel Red Bird and David Muskrat, members elect of the National Council, have been before the Cherokee people as public men many years. They have been proved and given satisfaction. They are in sympathy with the Administration and the chief.[21]

Ned Christie could speak fluently in English as well as in Cherokee, according to Harman. He became well known for his hot-tempered speeches on the legislative floor in defense of Cherokee sovereignty. Ever since the Civil War, the presence of intruders, as well as illegal whiskey, had been a continuing problem in the Cherokee Nation. Now movement was under way to open to white

---

*Records vary as to Nancy's age. Her tombstone lists her birthdate as 1871, the Cherokee Census of 1880 states her age at that time was ten, the Census of 1890 says she was 22.

Ned Christie, legislator and member of the Executive Council of the Cherokee Nation. *Copied, Daily Oklahoman, June 9, 1918.*

Tintype of Nancy Grease, left, second wife of Ned Christie, with kinfolks. *Courtesy John Christie.*

settlement a two million acre tract of land, known as the Unassigned Lands, in the heart of Indian Territory. Many were pressuring the Indians to take their lands in individual allotment, thus eliminate the tribes as separate nations. Those in power had to be constantly on guard to prevent this event from happening. Unfortunately, there were always those willing to sell out the Indian lands.

The leaders of the Cherokee Nation had long believed that one of the best means of safeguarding their future lay in the education of their young. Before the Civil War, the Cherokee schools had been the envy of the other tribes in Indian Territory and of the white settlers too. The male and female seminaries of higher education had been established in 1851 but were forced to close in 1856 because of lack of funds. They were not opened again until 1873. During the years they sat vacant, the two buildings fell into disrepair. Only recently had the Cherokee legislature appropriated funds to repair the two structures and place insurance on them.[22] The nation was shocked when the female seminary burned on April 10, 1887. Everyone expected it to be rebuilt at once.

Principal Chief Dennis Bushyhead immediately called the Executive Council into extra session to deal with the situation. When Councillors Ned Christie, Daniel Red Bird, and David Muskrat met on the morning after the fire, along with Executive Secretary William Boudinot and Interpreter William Eubanks, Chief Bushyhead presented them some bad news: for some unknown reason, the insurance on the female seminary had not been paid. The policy had been cancelled three days before the fire.[23] There was no money for rebuilding the seminary.

Stunned, the councillors discussed the problem. Chief Bushyhead presented a communication from Col. W.P. Ross, on behalf of the board of education in regard to carrying on the school during the present emergency. Finally, the councillors decided to adjourn until nine o'clock the following morning, at which time they would examine the various buildings available to house the female seminary until a new facility could be built.[24]

Meeting as planned, they toured the insane asylum, Col. Ross's primary recommendation, but decided they could not use this building for school purposes. None other seemed suitable. Returning to the legislative chambers, Chief Bushyhead proposed they present the matter to the entire National Council. The councillors agreed unanimously. Bushyhead set the date for the extra session to convene on May 9.[26] Thus the disastrous web of events, which was soon to entangle Ned Christie, was set in motion.

CHAPTER 2

Deputy Dan Maples and the Whiskey Problem

United States Deputy Marshal Daniel Maples lived near Bentonville, Arkansas,* sixty miles northeast of Tahlequah. A tall, husky man with patient, sad-looking eyes, he wore a thin handlebar mustache and scraggly beard. Shortly before the burning of the female seminary in the Cherokee Nation, Maples received a letter from Marshal John C. Carroll, U.S. District Court in Fort Smith. Carroll wanted Maples to make an immediate investigation of the whiskey-selling activities flourishing in and around Tahlequah in Indian Territory.[1]

A former sheriff of Benton County, Maples had done much to help clean up crime in the area and was well thought of. He had not been a deputy marshal long, nor had he made any arrests in Indian Territory so Carroll knew he would not be recognized there.[2] In addition, Maples was familiar with the difficult Cherokee language.[3] Known as an honest, dependable man, just the week before, Maples had arrested Bill Davis for postal robbery in Bentonville and lodged him in the Fort Smith jail.[4]

Maples was well aware of the liquor problem in Indian Territory. The Indian Intercourse Act of June 30, 1834, had expressly forbidden the selling or

---

*The headquarters for Sam Walton's Wal-Mart enterprise now occupies the former site of the Daniel Maples' farm, according to his great-granddaughter, Bettie Maples Halsell.

introduction of whiskey in Indian Territory. But four-fifths of the criminal cases in the Fort Smith court, which held jurisdiction over the violation of United States laws in the territory, were liquor related.[5] As the number of intruders in the region increased, the supply of whiskey became more plentiful.

In 1878, the Federal government authorized an underpaid Indian police force to deal with the liquor problem. The Indian police made a few arrests but little of the whiskey was destroyed, for the Cherokees opposed the law, and liquor-thirsty Indians shielded the whiskey peddlers, making it harder for the officers to run them down.[6]

In addition, whiskey profits were high and attracted tough and dangerous men. Whiskey bought on the Arkansas border for two dollars a gallon could be resold to the Indians for as much as twenty dollars. Many people were willing to take the chance of arrest for the high profits. If arrested, the fine for "introducing or attempting to introduce liquor in the Indian country," usually amounted to about five hundred dollars, while that for manufacturing ardent spirits was one thousand dollars.[7]

Most of the illegal liquor was smuggled in at the Arkansas border towns or through the railroad stations. Fort Gibson, fifteen miles west of Tahlequah, was known as a particularly vicious little town for liquor and outlaws. Fort Smith itself was a whiskey town, and the Moore brothers operated a large government distillery on the Arkansas border at Cincinnati.[8]

The principal offenders in "introducing and selling" liquor in Indian Territory were white men and women. So-called "whiskey marshals" operated throughout the territory, trying to combat the problem. Occasionally, they "spilled" some whiskey, but in the main the amber liquid continued to flow freely.

The editor of the *Fort Smith Elevator* complained that ninety-five percent of the crimes tried in the Fort Smith court from Indian Territory could be attributed to whiskey. He saw no solution to the problem short of disarming the Indians and backing Marshal Carroll's deputies with federal troops.[9]

Things had been particularly bad around Tahlequah of late. A near riot had occurred there in March, the result of a whiskey related problem. Thomas "Bub" Trainor, Jr., "a wild and reckless young man of the town," one of Tahlequah's "Saturday night outlaws," was the principal perpetrator of the incident.[10]

Trainor, nineteen, liked to get drunk and shoot up the town. He lived at the edge of town with his parents. Thomas Trainor, Sr., forty, was an expert buggy builder and blacksmith. Well-liked, he was known as a kind and loving husband except when he went on one of his occasional drunks. An adopted citizen of the Nation, he had come from Boston. When not under the influence of liquor, he was a quiet, useful citizen; when drinking, he was noisy but considered harmless.[11] Bub's mother, Lucy Trainor, forty, was a native Cherokee. She had served as a courier for Confederate officers during the Civil War.[12] Since then she and her husband had maintained close ties to the influential Boudinot, Stand Watie, and Bell families. Bub's brother, David, seventeen was enrolled in the male seminary while his sister, Anna,* attended the female seminary.[13]

Most of the citizens in town considered Thomas Trainor too indulgent where Bub was concerned, for Thomas had a tendency to overlook his son's wild ways and felt that local law officers were harassing him.

---

*Anna Trainor Bennett played the part of "Miss Indian Territory" in the mock wedding ceremony uniting the Twin Territories when Oklahoma became a state on November 16, 1907.

On Sunday evening, March 6, Bub and his wild young friends had been in town drinking again. They rode their horses up and down Muskogee Avenue, firing their guns, and forcing the stores to close in self-protection.[14] U.S. Deputy Marshal Jackson W. Ellis had been in the country squirrel hunting and just returned to town.[15] Five-eighths Cherokee, he was also captain of the Indian police stationed at Muskogee. These officers were appointed by the commissioner of the Indian agency of the Five Civilized Tribes. Considered U.S. peace officers, they commanded little respect from the Indians. The two successors of Ellis had been shot and killed in the line of duty the past year.

Ellis stopped Trainor on the street. "Bub, you better go on now and behave yourself," he advised.

Trainor took immediate offense. "You'd better get your gun," he told the law officer, "I've got mine."

Trainor rode down to Wilson's livery barn and put up his horse. He returned on foot up the middle of the street. Trainor wore a steel, bulletproof vest.[16] He drew on Ellis. Ellis returned his gunfire. Each got off three shots. One of Ellis' bullets hit Trainor in the center of the mouth, and the bullet lodged in the back of the young man's throat. Trainor fell to the ground.

The first ones to him, Ben Hartness, a seventeen-year-old Cherokee, and his brother, found Trainor about to drown in his own blood. They turned him over.[17]

"Oh, yes, God damn," Trainor said, "he shot at my teeth that time."

Hartness and his brother rubbed the blood out of Trainor's face. Ellis got Trainor's gun. He didn't want anyone else hurt, and he knew the Indians would go wild when they found Bub shot.

Some of Trainor's friends dragged him down the street to "Ballard's old store place." They sent for an Indian doctor close to Tahlequah. Pouring whiskey down Trainor, the doctor worked the bullet out of his mouth.

Trainor was lucky. Ellis had been shooting to kill but forgot he had been using some "little bulldog cartridges" in his Colt .45. These slugs were big enough to kill a squirrel and sometimes a man.[18]

Witnesses knew Bub Trainor had drawn first. Nevertheless, the peace officer's action provoked plenty of protest. "In a sense," stated the Vinita *Indian Chieftain*, "Ellis was besieged by the wounded man's friends."[19]

Ellis asked the U.S. Marshal's office in Fort Smith for assistance in restoring order in the town. John Hawkins, the High Sheriff of the national penitentiary and his guards, Than Woofard and Sam Manus, ordered a crackdown on Bub Trainor and his crowd.[20] Thomas Trainor complained that Hawkins was out to get his son. Bad blood had existed between the Trainor family and the law since then.

Marshal Carroll had sent a number of deputies to the area in an attempt to locate the source of illegal whiskey. So far, no one had found it. Now Maples had been handed the responsibility. Carroll suggested in his letter that he take as small a posse as possible to avoid suspicion. He enclosed a list of suspects, including the name of Bub Trainor, and advised Maples to contact U.S. Deputy Marshal Jackson Ellis at Fort Gibson for assistance.

To make the trip more profitable for Maples, Carroll also enclosed in the letter several warrants for other lawbreakers. A deputy operating in the territory received no salary, only fees and mileage. He received fifty cents for serving a paper, and two dollars for making an arrest. Expense money amounted to one dollar a day while chasing a person for whom he held a warrant, if he turned in the proper receipts. If he hired a posse or bought information, that money had to come out of his own pocket. If the deputy brought in his prisoner, he received ten cents a mile in allowances; if he killed his prisoner, he got nothing.

Carroll was well aware of the danger in chasing these whiskey peddlers. In a recent round letter published in the *Fort Smith Elevator*, he warned his deputies:

Don't ever underestimate a whiskey peddlar. It is a felony to sell whiskey to the Indians, and it is not the kind of a charge that most men would be willing to get into a shoot-out over. They come along peacefully enough once you catch them. But there is always that exception that a lawman must watch for at all times—if he intends to stay alive.[21]

Carroll had plenty of reason for concern. Since taking office on May 21, 1886, he had lost five deputies and four possemen who had been murdered in the line of duty.[22]

Maples knew the danger in accepting this assignment, but he considered himself a cautious, level-headed man and prepared to go. In accordance with Carroll's wishes, he kept his posse small. He chose two Bentonville men who had ridden with him before and proven trustworthy. George Jefferson, thirty-three, was a lean fellow of medium height with a clipped mustache. Mack Peel was the youthful son of Congressman Samuel W. Peel. Also riding with them was a young cook from Bentonville and Maples' oldest son, Sam.[23]

No trains ran directly into Tahlequah in those days. Lawmen usually made their circuit in wagons, carrying their camping equipment with them. When Maples' posse was ready to leave, the wagon carrying its supplies stood at the gate of Maples' home while the lawman bid goodbye to his wife, Maletha, and five younger children. Suddenly, a large crow flew down and landed on Maples' left shoulder. Though strongly religious, Maletha considered the bird an omen of

U.S. Deputy Marshal Daniel Maples was given the task of investigating illegal whiskey activities in Tahlequah in 1887. *Courtesy Phillip Steele and Mrs. Beatrice Maples Jones.*

Sam Maples, eldest son of Deputy Dan Maples and member of the posse led by his father. *Courtesy Phillip Steele.*

danger. She begged her husband not to go; she was afraid he would die. Maples laughed at her fears. Promising to be careful, he kissed her goodbye, and climbed into the wagon.[24]

As the five posse men traveled west, via the "Ridge Road," it seemed they were on the trip "more for pleasure and recreation than on business."[25] They gave the appearance of any of the hundreds of travelers passing through Indian Territory those days. The weather was cloudy and there was an unseasonable chill in the air— "blackberry winter," the Indians called it. The group reached Tahlequah late the second evening.

The town was situated in a well-watered and sheltered valley. The capital of the Cherokee Nation had been located here in 1839, following the removal of the Cherokees from the East. The capitol square lay in the middle of the town, and Muskogee Avenue, the main thoroughfare, ran past the capitol on the west side, and down a steep hill at the north end of town, where it crossed Spring Branch, which meandered through the town. A large spring, variously known as "Hendrick's Spring," or "Big Spring," fed Spring Branch on the north side. Sheltered by a grove of trees, the spring was a favored camping spot for travelers.

Beyond Big Spring, all but hidden among the trees, lay the seedier section of Tahlequah, "Dog Town." Here the less affluent citizens of the town lived. Several footlogs, which often washed away when the branch flooded, lay across Spring Branch, and one footpath trailed up the slope, past Big Spring and on to Dog Town while a second path curved westward beside the stream, at the foot of a chalk bluff. Maples and his posse made camp about one hundred yards above Big Spring.[26] That night it rained and the storm continued unabated the next morning. Maples determined to spend the day in camp.[27] This would soon prove to be a fateful decision.

CHAPTER 3

The Drinking Party

Ned Christie took his legislative duties seriously. Records show that ever since his election to the National Council in 1885, he faithfully attended every session of the law making body. During the week before the Special Session of the National Council to consider action pertaining to the burned female seminary, the Executive Councillors met daily in regular session to take care of the nation's general business.[1]

When in Tahlequah, it was Ned's habit to board at the home of Ned Grease, 1114 East Morgan. Grease, forty-two, was a relative of Nancy's father. A full-blood, he was one of the leaders of the National Party in the Tahlequah District, but he was looked upon by men of both political parties as worthy of trust.[2]

At the end of a busy day, Christie liked to go downtown after supper to find a drink of whiskey. Like most of the young Cherokee men, he had a fondness for the illegal drink, and, admittedly, sometimes drank too much. On December 24, 1884, he had been accused of killing a young Cherokee by the name of William Palone in a liquor-related incident.[3]

The affair happened in the Going Snake District, "at the cow camp of Leland Dick and his cowhands on the Caney, in the pigeon roost near the road leading from Gail Sixkiller's house to Step Preacher's." Palone died instantly from three Winchester shots.

The Going Snake sheriff arrested Christie and charged him with manslaughter. The motive for the

29

killing was believed to be an insult to Christie's mother.[4]

Christie pleaded not guilty and was brought to trial in the Going Snake court on May 24, 1885, with Judge Joel B. Mayes presiding. Six witnesses testified that Ned and his brother Jack had been present, among others, but no one admitted to seeing the actual shooting. After instruction by Judge Mayes, the jury returned a verdict of "not guilty."[5]

So Christie was well aware of the deadly combination of carrying weapons and ardent spirits. Principal Chief Bushyhead had spoken out sharply in regard to this issue in his last annual message to the Cherokee Nation.[6] In extra session the past spring, the National Council had discussed at length the growing liquor problem in the nation. Likely Christie recognized his own temperament. For the most part he was known to be a friendly, outgoing person with a cheerful disposition. But when intoxicated he could turn violent, if aroused, as the Palone incident indicated. On this evening of May 4, 1887, when he walked downtown looking for liquor, he left his gun at home, though he had been heard to say he felt naked without it.[7]

The evening was pleasant after the rain, which had continued most of the day, and Ned likely felt relaxed as he visited with friends on the street. Among them was a man named John Parris. A thirty-nine-year-old half-blood, Parris had come to Indian Territory with his parents during removal.[8] He and his wife Kate lived with seven children in Dog Town. Parris, along with his brothers George and James, had been in trouble with the Fort Smith court for many years. Their federal offenses ranged from stealing livestock to larceny, from assault with attempt to kill, to introducing and selling whiskey in Indian Territory.[9] Parris had served one year in the Federal House of Correction, Detroit, Michigan, for assault and had defaulted on a $1,000 bond for illegal whiskey operations. Kate had two charges of introducing and selling logged against her. Parris' name was also among those on the list of suspects that Marshal Carroll had given to Deputy Marshal Maples. Parris always knew where a drink could be found, and soon he and Christie could be seen heading towards Dog Town.

They crossed over the footlog on Spring Branch and walked up the slope past the wagon camped at Big Spring. They went directly to the cabin where Nancy Shell lived. Inside they found Bub Trainor, eating supper.[10]

Christie and Parris were well acquainted with Trainor, but right now they were more interested in obtaining a drink. Each bought a bottle of whiskey from Nancy Shell. She made a stopper for one of the bottles with a strip of cloth torn from her apron. She handed the bottle to Christie, who stuck it in an inside pocket of his black coat.[11]

Christie and Parris left the cabin. In the growing darkness at the edge of the woods, they met John Hogshooter, George Parris, and Charley Bobtail.

Bobtail, a full-blood, was an old offender like John and George Parris. On July 15, 1884, Bobtail had been sentenced to a term of eighteen months at the federal prison in Detroit for introducing and selling whiskey in Indian country.[12] Three months after his release, he was sentenced to another year in Detroit for horse stealing. Arriving home on March 24, he had immediately fallen in with his old companions.[13]

The five men drifted down the road. They stood talking near a house, then wandered toward upper Spring Branch where they continued laughing and drinking.

The moon came up. About 8:00 p.m., Christie said he was going back to his boarding house. He left the others and stumbled down the brushy path at the foot

Capitol of the Cherokee Nation where Ned Christie served as Executive Council member. *Courtesy of Cherokee Nation Historical Society.*

Students of the Cherokee Nation Female Seminary parade on Muskogee Avenue, Tahlequah. *Courtesy Western History Collections, University of Oklahoma Library.*

of the chalk bluff. As he neared the upper footlog, he collapsed into the bushes and passed out.[14]

Now all the characters who were to play out their part in the dramatic events which were about to change his life were on stage. But Christie slept on, oblivious to all.

CHAPTER 4

Murder at Big Spring

Late on Wednesday, when the sky began to clear, U.S. Deputy Marshal Maples and posse man George Jefferson crossed the footlog and walked downtown. A contemporary newspaper story describes Tahlequah as being a busy place with wagons rumbling up Muscogee Avenue, livestock wandering in the street, and chickens and geese pecking at grain sacks in the back of wagons hitched to the board fence which enclosed the capitol square. False-fronted buildings stood erratically spaced on both sides of the street, with a brick building interspersed here and there. A handful of soldiers from Fort Gibson wandered about among the other folks patronizing the stores. Few people paid any attention to the two law officers, for deputy marshals did not customarily wear their badges openly, and most men carried a gun.[1]

Maples unobtrusively inquired about the illegal whiskey operations in the area. In particular he was interested in suspects Bub Trainor and John Parris. Warrants were outstanding for each of them for introducing and selling whiskey.[2]

According to a story which appeared in the *Daily Oklahoman* in 1918, it was believed that Bub Trainor, in particular, was the most persistent supplier of illegal whiskey in Dog Town, especially to "Old Lady" Shell and "Old Mandy" Springston.[3] Maples soon learned that Shell lived in a cabin north of Big Spring.* Here she

---

*Located on today's southwest corner of Seminary Road and Smith Street, just west of Northeastern State University.

reportedly dispensed liquor and other favors. Bub Trainor was said to be a frequent visitor to her cabin.

Satisfied with what they had learned about the illegal whiskey sellers, Maples and Jefferson made their way to James S. Stapler's store, which was one of the oldest merchantiles in Indian Territory. Stapler also controlled the post office and the only telephone in town. Maples drew Stapler aside and told him he wanted to call the head marshal's office at Fort Smith, but that he did not want to talk until after Stapler had closed the store. Stapler replied that he would be doing so soon, as the day was drawing to a close. The *Daily Oklahoman* story continued:

> ...So the deputy walked out and went across the street to a hardware store where he loitered around for some time, then Stapler appeared at the door of the store and beckoned to the marshal to come over.
>
> Now, while Maples had been talking to Stapler when he first entered the store, there was a man who was making some small purchases at the counter. He overheard the conversation but pretended not [to] have heard. This man, who may be called Winn, was an associate of the 'tough' element of the town. As soon as his purchases were made he left the store, took his parcels to a house and returned to the street where he stood watching. When he saw Deputy Maples go back to the Stapler store from the hardware store Winn stepped into an alley and slipped up to the rear of the postoffice [sic] which was in the west end of the store. There was a tall plank fence just back of the rear window and behind this fence the man crouched and listened. Soon the officer was talking to the head marshal at Fort Smith. He requested that

warrants be immediately issued for the arrest of "Old Lady" Schell [sic] and "Old Mandy" Sprigston [sic], two notorious characters of the town who had been engaged in selling a good deal of firewater. As soon as the man crouched behind the fence heard these names mentioned he got up, slipped down the alley and made his way in a hurry to the home of [Senator] Bill Triplett. In this house there was the sound of dancing feet, ribald laughter, and squeaking of a fiddle. Winn dashed into the house and soon after Bud [sic] Trainor, a wild and reckless young man of the town, stepped out in his shirt sleeves with a big revolver stuck in his belt. He was followed by one Parris, a pressman in the old "Cherokee Advocate" office. What Parris did after coming out of the Triplett house is not stated, but Trainor made his way to the Tahlequah branch, a small creek flowing through the north part of town. When Trainor reached the creek he walked across to the other side on a footlog, and as he stepped to the bank of the creek he saw a man lying at full length in some small bushes near by.

As he lay in stupor, Bud [sic] Trainor, who wore a white shirt, stepped up to the sleeping man and drew the coat from his body. He put it on over his shirt and returning to the bank of the creek, took up his position behind a stooping tree. Revolver in hand, he waited and soon the officer came up from town and started to step upon the footlog. As he did so, Trainor fired. Just as he raised the weapon the deputy saw him and fired his own revolver. Trainor's bullet struck the marshal in the body and he fell mortally wounded, but so close did the officer's bullet come to the assassin that it clipped the neck from a bottle of whiskey that was in the inside pocket of the coat. The stopper of this bottle was a piece of the apron of "Old Lady" Schell [sic].[4]

Trainor's actions had not gone unnoticed. Further downstream on the lower footlog stood Richard A. "Dick" Humphrey, a fifty-six-year-old, blacksmith.[5] Humphrey had been brought to Indian Territory during Removal, from Georgia, with his parents as slaves of the Humphrey family. He and his parents were set free following the Civil War and adopted into the Cherokee Nation.[6] Humphrey settled on fourteen acres near Tahlequah, where he presently lived with his wife Emily, sixty, and their youngest daughter, Martha, twelve.[7] This evening Humphrey had been on his way to Dog Town and "Big Jennie's" shack, intent on obtaining a drink of moonshine before heading home after a hard day's work.

The air felt pleasant and a full moon lit the lower footlog as Humphrey started across. Then something moved upstream, and he paused, partially concealed by a bend in the creek. The *Daily Oklahoman* took up the story again:

> The old negro, when he saw Trainor take the coat from Christie and with revolver in hand stand behind the stooping tree, knew that there was going to be some desperate deed attempted or committed and as he, with others of the town, was afraid of Trainor, he did not care to be seen walking across the creek on the lower footlog. So he stood and watched and witnessed the assassination.[8]

He did not have long to wait. Dan Maples and George Jefferson soon came walking down Muskogee

Avenue, headed back to camp. They approached the upper footlog in the bright moonlight. As they did so, Trainor raised his gun. Jefferson, in advance of Deputy Maples, saw the muzzle of the pistol resting against the side of the tree on the opposite side of the branch. "Don't shoot!" he called out.[9]

But the assassin fired. The ball struck Maples in the right breast and tore its way out under his shoulder blade.[10] Maples fell, but recovered and drew his pistol. He fired at his enemy and missed.[11] Jefferson fired too. The three men emptied their weapons in quick succession.[12] Jefferson shouted to Peel, in camp at Big Spring, for help. Peel raced toward the footlog with gun in hand.

Trainor ran to Christie, threw his coat over him, shook him vigorously and told him to get up. Christie, half asleep, got to his feet, proceeded a short distance to a clump of small trees, lay down, and fell asleep again. Trainor left him there and rushed up the slope.[13] Peel "met a man making a hasty retreat, but not knowing that he was implicated in the shooting, let him pass."[14] Dick Humphrey, terrified by what he had seen, fled,* all thoughts of whiskey driven from his mind.[15]

The quick succession of shots at the upper end of the street were heard downtown. After a few minutes, someone brought the "startling word" that a deputy marshal had been waylaid and shot.[16] What marshal? A Mr. Maples of Bentonville, Arkansas. Then "it became

---

*Another reason which may have contributed to Humphrey not wanting to be involved in Ned Christie's case was the racial split which existed in the Cherokee Nation following the Civil War. The Cherokees were forced to take the freedmen into their tribe and share their land and annuities with them. Many of the Cherokees still resented this affair, and there was a division among the black and white bootleggers who lived in Dog Town, as well as among those who patronized them.

known that Maples was on his way to Fort Gibson and had gone into camp at Hendricks Spring because of the rain."[17]

The shooting soon attracted a large crowd to the banks of the branch.[18] Volunteers conveyed the wounded man back downtown to Dr. Blake, an old acquaintance of Maples. Here Maples received proper medical attention, but he was badly wounded.[19] Dr. Blake informed Sam Maples his father might not live. Sam started to Bentonville at once for his mother. But it was too late. Shortly after midnight, Deputy Maples died of internal hemorrhage.

Down by Spring Branch, Ned Christie slept on, blissfully unaware that the trouble, which had been stalking him for days, had finally arrived.

Spring Branch in the late 1880s, spanned by a
footbridge leading to Dog Town. *Courtesy Northeastern State University, Tahlequah.*

Big Spring, site of the murder of Deputy Daniel
Maples, as it appears today near Northeastern
State University in Tahlequah. *Photo by Bonnie
Speer.*

Citizens gather on the platform of an early store building which stood just south of the present telephone building on Muskogee Avenue in Tahlequah. Note board fence at the side of the store, and black man on the right. *Courtesy Western History Collection, University of Oklahoma Library.*

CHAPTER 5

The Charge

Ned Christie awoke in the pale light of dawn. He found himself lying on the bank of Spring Creek.[1] Feeling cold, he looked around for his coat. Unable to find it, he stumbled toward the footlog. The wagon camp above Big Spring looked strangely deserted.

He went back to town. There a friend met him and told him about the killing of Deputy Marshal Maples. He stated that Christie, John Parris, George Parris, John Hogshooter, and Charley Bobtail were all suspects as they had been seen on Spring Branch shortly before the shooting. Christie listened in amazement, and his friend suggested he leave town at once. Christie refused, for he said he knew nothing of the shooting.

He went to the boarding house where he discussed the matter with Senator Grease. Grease advised him to go on about his business, keep his mouth shut and wait for further developments.[2]

A large crowd collected downtown and there was great indignation among both whites and Indians over the killing of Maples. "Subsequent particulars of the tragedy" revealed that the murder was "one of the most wanton and dastardly crimes ever perpetrated in the Indian country," and "no cause could be assigned for the deed."[3]

"Many surmises were entertained as to the person who committed the deed and as to what purpose as Mr. Maples did not intend to arrest anyone at the place but was on his way to Fort Gibson at which place he had

42

phoned Jackson Ellis of the Indian Police and likewise the Deputy Marshal at Muskogee to meet him," said the Vinita *Chieftain*. "There is a belief he was killed through mistake as there has been much enmity between many of the citizens of the place and the high sheriff and his guard. Who was to blame for this it can be easily ascertained."⁴

George Jefferson told investigating officers that he had not seen the man who had shot at him and Maples. He and Mack Peel loaded the body of the murdered Maples into the back of the spring wagon and the men started the long, sad journey back to Bentonville, where Maples would be buried with Masonic honors.⁵

Early that morning, someone had sent a telegram to Marshal John Carroll in Fort Smith, informing him that Maples had been shot the previous night by "unknown parties" and had died a few hours afterwards of his wounds.⁶ Maples' death undoubtedly distressed Carroll more than usual, for not only had he lost another deputy, but he and Maples had been good friends, both socially and politically. The matter probably weighed heavily upon him as he walked down the hall to share with Judge Issac Parker the news of this latest fatality among his law keeping force.

On this day, the old federal building was unusually quiet. At the beginning of his tenure in 1875, Parker had established two court terms, one in May and the other in November. But because of the tremendous volume of cases in the court, the judge had merged the two terms into one with no apparent break. He convened the court at 8:30 a.m. and recessed at dark. Sometimes he held night court. He observed no holidays but Christmas and Sunday.⁷

Many people feared Parker, especially the Indians who appeared before him, feeling they had no chance at a fair trial before the strict judge. During his first court term, Parker had tried ninety-one criminals. Of eighteen murder cases, fifteen had ended in conviction and six of the defendants had been hanged. More knowledgeable people considered Parker an able lawyer and jurist. They knew that in his mind, the most extreme violation of the law was the killing of an officer of the law. He believed that without the inviolability of the court and its marshals, there could be no law, and he exhibited little patience toward those who killed one of his deputies.[8]

The May term of 1887 had opened three days before on the second, but the court had already run into one of its periodic lack of funds, and the wheels of justice, as far as jury trials were concerned, had ground to a halt. The "occupants of the marshal's and clerk's offices rested easy, gathering energy for the busy work in July," for new operating funds would not be available until that time.[9] It seemed an opportune moment, and Marshal Carroll decided to go to Tahlequah to take personal charge of the investigation concerning his friend's death.

He caught a train to Fort Gibson and arrived in Tahlequah late that evening. He met with Deputy Marshal John Curtis who was conducting the preliminary investigation. Curtis told him all he knew of the shooting. He related that as he and his assistants were searching the scene of the killing, near the tree behind which the assassin had stood, they found the neck of a whiskey bottle which Curtis surmised might have been shot off during the fight. The bottle had an unusual stopper, one made from a torn strip of cloth.

A subsequent search led the officers to the home of Nancy Shell. She admitted that the piece of cloth had been torn from her apron. She said she had sold the bottle to John Parris and Ned Christie. The two had left her place a short time before the shooting, "considerably drunk."[10]

Curtis had arrested Nancy Shell and Julia Bell for selling bootleg whiskey. He held John Parris for questioning, but he had not been able to locate Ned Christie.

Carroll took over the investigation and interrogated John Parris. Parris admitted to having been in the area at the time of the shooting, but denied committing the murder and refused to identify his companion. Carroll could find nothing concrete on which to hold Parris in regard to the murder. However, he warned him to stay in the area, and served him with a subpoena on the old charge of skipping bond on November 19, 1885. Carroll noted carefully on the back of the warrant, "...this is a true copy of the original at Fort Smith, Ark..."[11]

Curtis told Carroll that many people believed that John Hawkins or Jackson Ellis had been the intended victim.[12] Curtis gave Carroll a rundown on the trouble, which had existed since March, between the two law officers and Bub Trainor. Both agreed that Trainor was also a likely suspect.

Next morning, Curtis and Carroll once again combed the scene of the killing. In the bushes beside Spring Branch, they found a black coat with a bullet hole in it and the remains of the broken whiskey bottle. Learning of this, the *Fayetteville Democrat* reported there were "strong indications that the clue has been hit upon."[13] Ned Grease heard the rumor and knew things looked bad for Christie. He urged him to leave town at once. Christie objected, repeating that he knew nothing of the killing. He said he did not shoot the deputy, that he did not even have a gun with him at the time of the incident.[14] But Grease knew that while many considered Christie an honorable, upright citizen, they would remember also the shooting of William Palone.

The *Fort Smith Elevator* related that on Saturday evening, the "good citizens of Tahlequah held an indignation meeting." At the meeting they passed the following resolutions:

> Resolved that we the undersigned citizens of Tahlequah deeply deplore the recent murder in our midst and our heartfelt sympathy is hereby extended to his friends and loved ones at home in the great loss they have sustained.
> Resolved further that we bitterly condemn and abhor the commission of so terrible and unusual a crime within our midst and we ask the principle [sic] chief to use what means he has in his power to arrest the guilty party and deliver him to the proper authority in conformity with the intercourse laws of the United States which by treaty are made obligatory on us.[15]

The resolutions were signed by a great many of the citizens, with Chief Bushyhead's signature heading the list. Bushyhead offered a reward of $300 for the arrest of the slayer of Maples. In addition, the citizens of Tahlequah made up a private reward, promising to do all in their power to catch the slayer and bring him to trial.

On Monday morning, the extra session of the General Council convened. Refusing to be intimidated by the many rumors about the slaying of Maples, Ned Christie attended Chief Bushyhead's opening speech.[16] Like always, this meeting was held outdoors on the southwest corner of the public square so all could hear. Afterwards the legislators entered the capitol to take up the business of rebuilding the female seminary.

But before the day ended, word came to Christie that the suspect coat which had been found had been identified as his and that he was going to be charged in federal court with the murder of Maples. "Becoming excited, he slipped away and rode home to his family."[17]

Behind him, Dick Humphrey, the blacksmith, held his silence, too frightened of Bub Trainor and his gang (and perhaps of racial prejudice?) to come forward and tell what he knew.[18]

CHAPTER 6

State's Evidence

Ned Christie was in a truly dangerous position, as he was to soon find out. Writs had been obtained in federal court for his arrest and that of John Parris, Bub Trainor, Charley Bobtail, and George Parris. All were charged with involvement in the murder of Deputy Maples.

On Tuesday evening, May 17, Deputy Marshal John Curtis arrived in Fort Smith with Charley Bobtail in custody. "If he is not the one who did the actual killing," reported the *Fort Smith Elevator* "he does not deny being with the other parties charged with the crime, but says John Parrish [sic] is the man who did the fatal shooting....Writs are out for three others besides John Parish [sic], who will be brought in before a great while."[1]

The *Elevator* had plenty of reason to be optimistic. Marshal John Carroll had sent Deputy Marshal "Heck" Thomas, one of his best officers, after the other three wanted men.

A native Georgian and well educated, at the age of twelve, Heck Thomas had served as courier for his uncle, Gen. Edward Lloyd Thomas, in the 35th Georgia Volunteers during the Civil War. During the turbulent reconstruction period, Thomas won distinction as a member of the Atlanta police force, though not yet eighteen years of age. In 1876, he moved to Texas, where, two years later, he gained fame by outwitting the noted outlaw Sam Bass during a robbery attempt.[2]

A dead shot, Thomas joined the marshal's office in Fort Smith late in 1885. His reputation as a persistent and crafty lawman spread rapidly. He always went after the most dangerous outlaws, stayed longer in the field, and brought in more prisoners at a time than any other deputy.[3]

True to expectation, on Saturday, May 21, about 9:00 p.m., Deputy Marshal Heck Thomas and Sam Wingo arrived at the Fort Smith jail with John Parris and another prisoner, named Harvey Dale, who had been charged with breaking into a store at Fort Gibson.[4]

"Should he [Parris] prove to be the right man," stated the *Muskogee Indian Journal*, "he [Heck Thomas] will have made a very profitable haul, as there is a $500 reward for the murderer."[5]

Reportedly, on the authorization of Chief Bushyhead, the high sheriff had made the arrest and turned Parris over to Deputy Heck Thomas.[6]

"Of course he [Parris] denies all complicity in the Maples murder," said the *Fort Smith Elevator* "and will no doubt get an opportunity to prove his innocence. Other arrests are looked for at any time."[7]

But the other suspects were not to be taken so easily. Like all Indians, they feared the white man's court. Though the Treaty of 1866 had granted them right of jurisdiction over their own lands and people, federal authorities in Arkansas had persisted for years in sending officers into Indian Territory to arrest the Indians and drag them back across the line. Here the prisoners might lie for weeks and months in jail, ignorant of their legal recourse. The Indians complained bitterly at the violation of their rights but to no avail.

Following an act of March 3, 1885, the federal court claimed jurisdiction in Indian Territory over certain cases involving any Indian, including "murder, manslaughter, rape, assault with intent to kill, arson, burglary and larcency," on or off the reservation.[8]

In 1887, this law had been further strengthened by a second mandate which stated that "any Indian committing murder, manslaughter or assault with intent to kill against any Indian enforcement or police officer in Federal service should be subject to the laws of the United States and be tried in the United States courts having jurisdiction where the crime was committed."[9]

Ned Christie discussed his situation with Robin Vann, a member of the Cherokee Indian Police. Christie told him that he "absolutely did not shoot Maples," but that if Vann believed he had murdered the lawman, he would give himself up to the Indian police and stand trial in the Cherokee Nation.[10]

But Vann told Christie that the Cherokee police had no complaint against him and he did not wish to make the arrest. So Christie, "having knowledge of the feelings of the Cherokees, did not go to his home but lingered among friends and neighbors who helped him to avoid the United States marshals who watched for his return home day and night. It was said every Cherokee who knew him believed he did not kill Maples, but John Parris."[11]

The editor of the *Tahlequah Telephone* accused Principal Chief Bushyhead of openly flouting the federal law and of protecting a murderer, for George Parris could not be found, while Bub Trainor, heavily armed, "can be seen on our streets ever day."[12]

On May 30, United States Deputy Marshals Bud Kell, Jackson Ellis, and Blue Foreman asked United States Commissioner J.W. Tufts at Muskogee to swear out an additional warrant for Trainor.[13]

The warrant charged Trainor, "on or about the 6 day of March, 1887," with assaulting Indian Deputy U.S. Marshal and Indian Policeman J.W. Ellis with a deadly weapon with intent to kill. Commissioner Tufts noted on the back of the warrant: "He [Trainor] is the same one wanted for murder of Maples but may not be held on that charge. Kell & Ellis things [sic] he can get him."[14]

When Thomas Trainor, Sr., heard about this latest warrant for his son's arrest, he angrily denounced the officers for what he considered the continued harrassment of his son. His half-blood friends took up the cry, and the situation in Tahlequah became volatile as rumors spread. The *Siloam Springs Herald* reported:

> Two companies of military have been ordered to Tahlequah by the government to quiet the Cherokees. It seems that things have been running in very bad order since the killing of Maples and it is reported that someone "thought to have been connected with the killing of Maples" shot into Chief Bushyhead's house a few days ago and after this the Chief telegraphed for the military to be sent there. Two pieces of artillery are planted in the town. Uncle Sam will quell the matter.[15]

E.B. Stone, the outspoken editor of the *Tahlequah Telephone*, which had begun publication on May 12, reprinted the *Herald* article and indignantly denied the report:

> There is not a word of truth in any so far of the above insertion. The People of the Nation, and especially in and around Tahlequah regret the killing of Maples very much and are doing all that is in their power to bring the guilty parties to justice. Their motto is "Let the guilty man hang." Should we need the military you only have to telephone to Fort Gibson and we can have them here in four hours.[16]

In the midst of all the turmoil, the Cherokee National Council had closed its special session on May 24 after appropriating $60,000 for rebuilding the female seminary above Hendricks Spring where Deputy Dan Maples had been shot. Records show that Ned Christie dared not appear after the first day, for fear of being arrested. Chief Bushyhead ordered the Executive Councilors to meet again in Special Session on June 27, and once more Ned Christie was noticeably absent.[17]

Across the street, Thomas Trainor, Sr., continued to brood about his son. On Thursday, June 20, he began drinking. About sundown he approached Evans Drug Store, located next door to Stapler's store.[18] On the platform before the store sat High Sheriff John Hawkins and Than Wooford, visiting with J. Hooper, Johnson Parris and James Trainor. As servants of the law, Hawkins and Wooford were both armed. Witnesses later stated that Thomas Trainor suddenly saw Hawkins as the source of all his son's trouble with the law. Walking up behind Wooford, Trainor jerked Wooford's pistol from his belt, and aimed at Hawkins. "Now I've got you," he declared.[19]

Hawkins immediately drew his own pistol. Several shots were fired. Thomas Trainor fell, shot through the abdomen. A crowd collected immediately, and witnesses were divided as to which man had fired first.[20] But all agreed, Trainor had taken the pistol from Wooford and aimed at Hawkins. Trainor was carried to his residence where he died the next morning about ten o'clock, begging forgiveness for his act.[21]

Because Thomas Trainor was a white man, High Sheriff Hawkins was arrested and taken before United States Commissioner Tufts at Muskogee. He was examined along with witnesses J. Hooper, Johnson Parris, and James Trainor before being discharged.[22]

On the same day that Thomas Trainor was shot, Deputy Marshal John Curtis arrested "one Hogshooter and one Bobtail, the latter a brother to Charley Bobtail in the Fort Smith jail for complicity in the murder of Dan Maples,"[23] along with three women, charging them with introducing and selling whiskey in the Indian country. He lodged his prisoners in the Fort Smith jail where John Parris and Charley Bobtail languished in the crowded, ill-lighted and airless room beneath Judge Parker's courtroom, which was often compared to the "Black Hole of Calcutta," by those who survived it.

Upstairs, the court was still in its periodic slump because of the lack of funds. It was not until the end of June that the marshal's and clerk's offices began to gear up for the expected activity. Parris' attorneys, Mellet and Barnes, arrived to confer with him.[24] When the court reconvened on July 5, the docket listed an unusually heavy load, including twenty-four murder cases. The grand jury docket listed twelve murder cases. Among these was the case of Charles Bobtail, John Parris, George Parris, Bub Trainor, and Ned Christie who were all charged with the murder of Deputy Marshal Dan Maples.[25] Several hundred witnesses and other court attendants from all parts of Indian Territory thronged the courtyard and were still coming in as the legal wheels of justice began to turn.[26]

On July 9, Nancy Shell pleaded guilty to being a retail liquor dealer without a license and was remanded to the custody of Marshal Carroll to wait final sentence.[27] Deputy Marshal Heck Thomas arrived with George Parris in tow on July 20.[28] Three days later, the grand jury called case No. 2021. It found a true bill of indictment against John Parris, Charley Bobtail, Bub Trainor, and Ned Christie for the murder of Deputy Marshal Dan Maples.[29]

Arraigned before the court, Parris and Bobtail pleaded not guilty and were held for trial. Since Ned Christie and Bub Trainor had "not yet appeared or pleaded," the court ordered Marshal Carroll to issue writs for their immediate arrest and to bring them before the court on the first day of August.[30]

On the same day, the grand jury issued a second indictment against Bub Trainor for "introducing liquors in the Indian Country."[31] He had been arrested the day before in Tahlequah by Deputy Sheriff Roach of the tribal police, but for some reason had not been turned over to federal officers. Instead, he was released.[32]

In anticipation of his trial, John Parris immediately filed a subpoena for witnesses at court expense. He stated that without the testimony of Ned Grease, Steve Vann, Mrs. Eva Thorn, John Hogshooter, and Lafayette Guinn, all of whom lived at or near Tahlequah, he could not safely proceed to trial.[33]

By these witnesses, Parris swore that he could "prove that at the time Deputy United States Marshal Maples was killed he was about a quarter of a mile from the place of the killing," and "at the time the shot was fired...Vann, Grease, and Hogshooter were talking to him or were near him, and that defendant was entirely unarmed."[34]

His trial was set for October 5, along with that of Charley Bobtail. At that time, John Parris promised to turn state's evidence. He claimed that Ned Christie was the guilty party. He related that he and Christie had met Maples when drinking at the spring. Christie had accused Maples of stealing. A fight had ensued and Christie shot and killed Maples.[35]

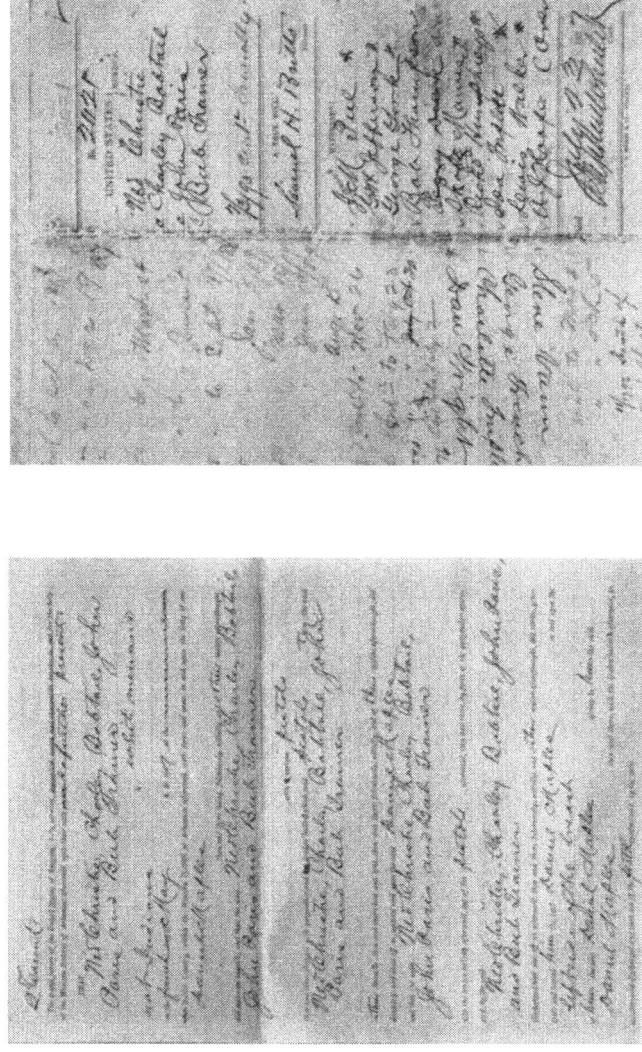

Warrant for the arrest of Ned Christie, Charley Bobtail, John Parris, and Bub Trainor, all charged with the murder of Deputy Daniel Maples. Note that posse men J. M. Peel and George Jefferson were called as witnesses, as well as Richard Humphrey (fourth name from the bottom), eyewitness to the murder of Maples. The case was continued from term to term as shown on the left, and closed with the death of Ned Christie. *Copied from original warrant in Federal Archives and Record Center, Fort Worth.*

CHAPTER 7

The Battle Begins

When word of Ned Christie's indictment for murder reached Rabbit Trap, his father, Watt Christie, and several members of the National Council brought pressure on him to surrender and stand trial. Ned refused, he said he knew who had killed Maples but would not tell.[1]

Finally he decided "the honorable thing to do was to write a letter to Judge Parker, explaining that he did not kill Maples."[2] In the letter he stated that he would surrender if Judge Parker would allow him bond so that he could go about unmolested and accumulate evidence to prove his innocence.[3]

He showed the letter to Timothy Brown Hitchcock, who lived several miles north of Rabbit Trap on Barren Creek. Three-eighths Cherokee, Hitchcock served as clerk of the Cherokee Senate. His father and two uncles had come to the Cherokee Nation in 1824 when Fort Gibson had been established.[4]

Hitchcock deemed the letter was a good one. It was delivered to "two prominent Tahlequah citizens" who had volunteered to take it to Fort Smith. The two men "went on two occasions" to Fort Smith to talk to the famous "hanging judge" and the court officials. But they found "everyone had fully decided that Christie was the guilty one and that he positively could expect no bond." In addition, "it was nearly a daily occurrence to kill a U.S. marshal and Judge Parker was determined that the practice must be stopped, if he had to hang every outlaw in the Cherokee Nation."

When Ned Christie heard this report, he vowed he would never go to Judge Parker's court to be hanged, that he would rather die at home fighting.[5]

As soon as he made this decision, Christie sent for his brother-in-law, Seed Wilson. The husband of Rachel, Ned's olderst sister, Seed lived near Locust Grove in the Sequoyah District and was a medicine man. The Cherokees placed great faith in their medicine men. Such a person was set aside and consecrated to his calling from birth. It was said that he believed deeply in spiritual things. He sensed the place where thoughts were coming from, and listened to the voice of nature in the roar of thunder and heard the voice of the Great Spirit in the whisper of the wind. The wisdom of the medicine man was regarded as profound, his spells potent, and his knowledge highly secret. He could "make tobacco," that is confuse the thoughts of witnesses in a courtroom, or help prisoners escape. He could heal the sick and wounded with his special herbs.[7]

Seed Wilson spent three weeks with Christie in a secret place in the woods, going through his ceremonies and placing a "spell" on him. At the end of this time Christie returned home, confident the deputy marshals could not catch him now.[8]

His faith was soon tested. One morning he saw a lawman trying to slip up on his cabin. Christie stepped to the door with his gun in hand. The deputy marshal started to run. Christie fired to scare him, and struck the man in the heel, but he kept running.[9]

A second time, while Christie was eating breakfast, he heard the warning, "Someone coming in gate." Again he stepped to the door with his gun, and when the lawman turned to run, Christie fired, his bullet striking the fleeing officer in the neck.[10]

This made two more counts against Christie for resisting arrest and assaulting a deputy, though it was said that he "did not shoot to kill, but to make them quit sneaking around his house."[11] After this incident,

Christie's friends and relatives in the Keetoowah set up a system of signals in the neighborhood to warn him when danger was near.

The Keetoowah Society had originated nearly 200 years earlier. Its purpose was to protect the full-blood Cherokees against aggression, and especially to guard their political and civil rights. The name Keetoowah meant the "Real People," or "Principle People."[12]

The Keetoowah had languished following Removal but was reorganized in 1859. The members were all full-bloods with a national feeling of patriotism. Almost without exception during the Civil War they had gone with the North. They had secret passwords and wore an insignia of two crossed pins on the left coat lapel, for which they were often called "Pin Indians." They held secret rituals in the woods and kept the eternal fire of the Cherokees burning in the tribal council house. They protected the sacred wampum belt, which related the history of the Cherokee tribe from its early beginnings, and the seal of the original Keetoowah Society.

Following the Civil War a few half-bloods and adopted citizens had been taken into the Keetoowah. In recent years there had been dissension among them with a group calling themselves the "Night Hawks" threatening to split, for they were in favor of allotment of the Cherokee lands and dissolution of the Cherokee tribal government, which the full-bloods opposed. All could be counted upon, however, in time of trouble.

Some time in the past, the Keetoowah had built a lookout tower on Spade Mountain so they could watch for white men. Now they set up a system of signals there to warn Ned Christie when the deputy marshals were in the area. Each time the lawmen appeared, Christie disappeared into the woods.

Meantime, the executive council continued its regular monthly meetings during July and August with Ned Christie still absent. Nagged by the neglect of his duties, he finally sent notice to Chief Bushyhead that he wanted to submit his resignation. The council met on August 24 to consider his request, and decided that the "public interests demanded that the position of Executive Councilor held by Edward Christie should be declared vacant on account of his absence without explanation from his post of duty since May last, he being evidently unable or disabled from serving." William Eubanks was appointed to fill the vacancy.[13]

In all likelihood, Christie's strong voice and dominant personality were sorely missed in the legislature. The movement to open the Unassigned Lands to white settlement was gaining popularity in the United States Congress. Many tribal members were urging that the Cherokees take their lands in severalty and individual allotments, and to join with the Chickasaws, Choctaws, Seminoles, and Creeks to form a separate state in the union. Others argued, "the very moment the Cherokees go into confederation, they lose their identity as an intelligent race of Indians..." Rabbit Bunch accused the Downing party of wanting the individual allotment bill passed and cautioned those in the National party to be careful whom they sent to the legislature, else the bill would be enacted into law.

The general election on August 1 had ended in dispute with Rabbit Bunch of the National party and Joel B. Mayes of the Downing party each claiming enough votes to be elected for Principal Chief. There were rumors that the dominate National party might fail to call a joint meeting to settle the dispute. Ned's father, Watt Christie, had lost his seat in the National Council during the election, and charges of graft and corruption were being hurled at those remaining in office.

In the midst of this turmoil, Editor Stone of the *Tahlequah Telephone* was still slinging accusations at local law officer stating that they were allowing U.S.

citizens to be murdered and claiming that they were making no attempt to arrest the guilty parties. He accused:

> These murderers could have been promptly arrested and turned over and it would have shown a disposition on our part to do the fair thing. It would have shown we did not countenance such deeds and that we were acting in good faith to our superior government... Mr. Bushyhead could have raised self in estimation of citizens...if he had forced the officers of the law to carry out the law.[14]

Whether Stone was referring to the death of Deputy Marshal Maples or that of Thomas Trainor, Sr., is not clear, but on September 20, Deputy Connelly lodged High Sheriff John Hawkins and Deputy Sam Manus in jail for the murder of Trainor.[15]

Hawkins had been examined previously for the murder by Commissioner Tufts and dismissed, but during the past week, the grand jury in the federal court in Fort Smith, had indicted both Hawkins and Manus for the murder. Why Manus was indicted was uncertain, stated the *Fort Smith Elevator*, "for it was said Manus was not even present at the killing."[16] Hawkins posted a $1,000 bond and Manus was committed to jail. Manus was a half-blood from the Going Snake District and married to Ned Christie's sister, Mary.

In Fort Smith, the Maples murder case was continued until December as Bub Trainor and Ned Christie were still at large. John Parris filed a motion for additional witnesses, this time calling for Mary Guinn, Josie Shell, and Looney Coon, by whom he said he could prove he was "about a quarter of a mile from where the shooting took place and that he was not in anywise engaged in it.[17]

National Historic Site of the Federal Court of the Western District of Arkansas, Fort Smith. Judge Parker's court was located on the first floor and the jail, which was compared to the "Black Hole of Calcutta," was in the basement. *Photo by Bonnie Speer.*

Judge Issac Parker, federal court judge, Fort Smith, considered the unpardonable sin as being the killing of a U.S. deputy marshal. *Courtesy Western History Collections, University of Oklahoma Library.*

Meanwhile, Bub Trainor was stirring up more trouble. On September 25, his gang engaged in a row with that of Dick Vann on Fourteen Mile Creek. The Vann outlaws had been visiting Fort Gibson and "painting the town red." The Trainor gang robbed Vann of his pistols and whiskey, and "severely pounded him."[18]

On October 8, the Trainor gang entered Oaks, a small settlement north of Tahlequah, where they were accused of burning "a Store House, the property of one Lafayette Duckworth, a white." A writ was subsequently issued for the arrest of Bub Trainor, John Leach, Joseph Miller, and William Chuis on incendiary charges.[19] Chuis and Miller were jailed on October 28, and on November 19, Deputy Marshal Jackson W. Ellis finally arrested Bub Trainor for "Murder in the Indian Country, Introducing and selling and Assault with intent to kill."[20]

Trainor hired a very able attorney to secure his release. The half-blood son of Elias Boudinot, who was a member of the Treaty party and the first editor of the *Cherokee Phoenix* and the *Cherokee Advocate*, Elias C. Boudinot was described as "a grand fellow, above average in height, stalwart, well formed."[21] A former Cherokee delegate to the Confederate Congress during the Civil War, promoter of Vinita and of the first railroad through Indian Territory, he was alternately termed a visionary and a rogue. He was but a boy when his father was murdered in June 1839 for participating in signing away by treaty Cherokee lands in the East for those in the West. But Boudinot's bitterness over this had grown until he became obsessed with the idea of destroying the influence of the Ross party (or the National party as it was later called), which he held responsible for his father's death.

He had been advocating a territorial government for Indian Territory since 1865, with the holding of land in severalty. In 1879, he published an article in the *Chicago Times* stating that the Unassigned Lands in Oklahoma were public domain and subject to homesteading, thus setting off a furor along the frontier among land-hungry settlers and initiating the Boomer movement in Kansas.[22] Having close ties to the Trainor family, on December 5, 1887, Boudinot appeared before the court with Bub Trainor, who pleaded not guilty to all charges against him. Trainor was bound over for trial in March and was released in January on $6,500 bond. Meanwhile, the quest to arrest Ned Christie continued in Rabbit Trap.

CHAPTER 8

Another Charge

For the most part, Rabbit Trap was a pleasant place to live. An article published in September 1885 in the *Cherokee Advocate*, described the area, located in the center of the Going Snake District, as being "bountifully supplied" with sparkling springs. The story said fine crops of corn, stacks of wheat, and fields of oats greeted the visitor on every side, and numerous cattle grazed in the district.[1]

Men cultivated their land with "crude deer tongues of wood" or a single stock plow hitched to oxen with rough harness, built hand-hewn rail fences and hunted in the woods.[2] The women cooked outside over a "chunk fire" when the weather was hot, and when cooler, on an indoor fireplace. They made bright-colored, loose-fitting hunting shirts for the men and crafted baskets and pottery to be traded in Arkansas at Dutchtown, Cincinnati, and Siloam Springs.[3]

Deer, wild turkeys, rabbits, quail, and prairie chickens abounded in the area. Bear roamed the Walkingstick Mountains. Golden eagles ranged over Black Bean Mountain, Caney Ridge, and Hungry Mountain. Residents reported two major passenger pigeon roosts in the region, one north of Rabbit Trap on the Barren Fork, and the other four miles south on the Caney.[4] The birds were so numerous all believed they would exist indefinitely.*

---

*Before the close of the 1880s, the passenger pigeons were becoming scarce. Several more years and they were gone. The

The families of Rabbit Trap took their corn to the Bitting water mill to be ground into meal.* They traded at Levi Keys' store at Wauhillau, which was located a mile and a half south of Bitting Spring, on the main road from Fort Smith to Fort Gibson. Keys carefully documented everything, including the exchange of the cow which Ned Christie took out in trade that spring.[5]

The schools and churches in the Going Snake District were the center of social life and community gatherings. The Indians attended ceremonial dances on John Wolf's place near Wauhillau, and sometimes the men held a cornshoot. The elderly spent much time chatting about the old days back East. The young people popped corn, made molasses candy, and cracked nuts.

But there was another side of the Going Snake District which was not so pleasant. It was a wild country with no quick transportation, so horse thieves, whiskey peddlers, and other outlaws sought safety in the isolated hills. Killings were frequent. A man named Stephens bootlegged whiskey at his small mill on the Caney, and many drunken Indians roamed the area.[6]

U.S. deputy marshals made a circular tour through the area before each term of federal court.[7] They hauled their prisoners back to Fort Smith in a wagon, chaining the men to it, or to a tree at night like animals. None of the deputies had come close to Ned Christie yet. He seemed to have a sixth sense about danger. Some said

---

last flocks were seen roosting on the banks of Barren Fork near Welling. The Cherokees believed the pigeons had attempted to cross the ocean or were caught in a tornado because they left one day and never returned.

*Later known as Golda's Mill, this facility was in operation until November 1987, when it burned.

he could smell a rattlesnake when it lay coiled and ready to strike. When a deputy marshal did manage to get close, Christie fired a warning shot to let him know he had been seen, and gobbled at him.

The Cherokee gobble was peculiarly Indian. An unearthly sound, it was described as being something between the howl of a coyote and the gobble of a turkey.[8] The Indians used it in defiance against an antagonist. A defendant once pleaded before Judge Parker that he had killed another Indian because the man had gobbled at him. The prosecutor was aghast at the flippancy of the excuse until the defendant introduced several witnesses who testified that when an Indian gobbled, he meant sudden death to any and all in his path.[9]

During the Civil War, the full-bloods in the Union Army had gobbled lustily when setting out on expeditions. Uttered in unison, the gobble produced a great volume of sound, rising above the roar of the artillery. Supposedly the noise so terrified their Confederate opponents it often caused them to fall into disorder. Just when the Cherokees began using the gobble no one knows.[10]

In his isolation at Rabbit Trap, Ned Christie brooded over his situation. News from the outside trickled into the community. He heard that on January 4, 1888, following the regular session of the National Council, some members of the Downing party sallied forth with their Winchesters to end the political deadlock which had existed since the last election, and overpowered the National guard at the capitol.[11] Hooley Bell kicked in the door of the executive office where Chief Bushyhead still sat in power, put him out, and administered the oath of office to Joel B. Mayes. United States officials called for an investigation but nothing had come of it, and the new administration continued harmoniously in power. Christie angrily watched the situation, unable to do anything.

The more he thought about his situation, the more he drank. He made arrangements for his bootleg whiskey to be shipped to Bunker station on the train. On Sunday morning, February 19, 1888, when Christie arrived to pick up his shipment, the station agent informed him that Bear Grimmet had already obtained it. If he hurried, he could catch up with him.[12]

Bear Grimmet was considered one of the worst outlaws in the territory. He hid out at Robber's Roost in the Cookson Hills south of Rocky Mountain. He had killed Pet Hawk there and Deputy Marshal Beck on Big Sallisaw Creek northwest of Sallisaw. After this incident Grimmet had become a desperado in a big way. He and his men regularly peddled whiskey in the area, replenishing their supply at the Arkansas border and returning to their hideout.[13]

Christie and a companion named Joe Eagle set out after Grimmet. They caught up with him on the road to Sallisaw near George Scott's home in the Flint District. With Grimmet were Rat Panther and Saddle Blanket. Bill Blair, Taylor Christie, Jess Pigeon, and George Lanaheate were also present. Within a few minutes, Grimmet lay dead in the road and the others scattered.[14]

Because all the participants were Indian, the Cherokee Nation assumed jurisdiction in the case. Sheriff's deputies arrested Pigeon, Blair, and Taylor Christie. A preliminary hearing convened in the Flint courtroom on March 5. The three prisoners were released and called as witnesses along with Saddle Blanket and several others. Saddle Blanket testified:

> Joe Eagle shot Bare [sic] Grimmet twice and Ned Christie helped him to shoot Bare Grimmet. When Joe Eagle came up to Bare Grimmet he talked a good deal, Joe Eagle say we are all friends though maybe you are afraid of me and

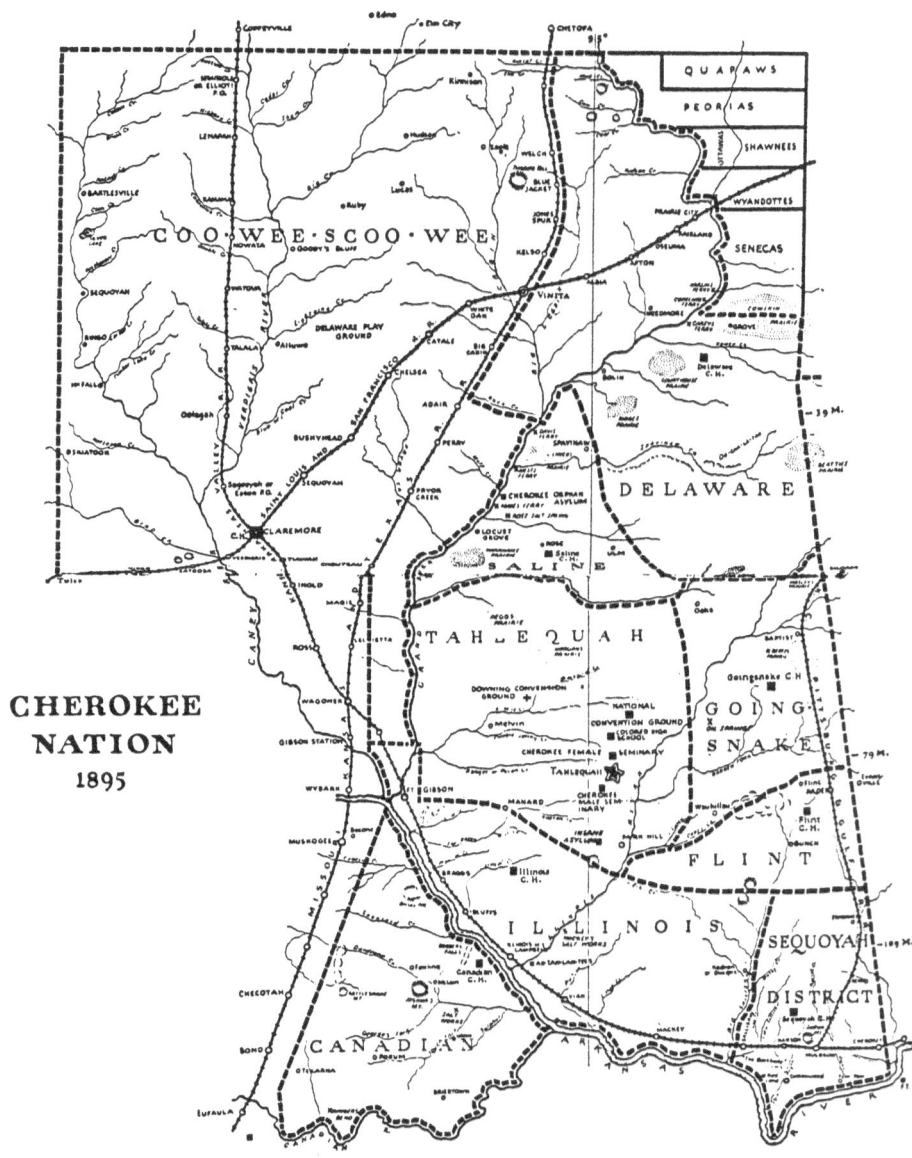

CHEROKEE
NATION
1895

Map of the Cherokee Nation in 1895. The Rabbit Trap
community was located in the Going Snake district,
near Wauhillau.

he went around to where we was standing, and he then shot Bare below the shoulder, and Bare sunk down and he then shot him again and then run. When I run I heard some one of them say go kill Saddle Blanket, too.[15]

Under questioning by the solicitor, Saddle Blanket said he did not see anyone else in the crowd draw a weapon. He related that his party had stayed all night at Mrs. Vann's and were on their way home when they met Taylor Christie and Blair. Then Pigeon and Lanaheate came along, both riding the same horse. They stopped about twenty steps away from the others. Further testimony established that Ned Christie and Joe Eagle had arrived together. Eagle stopped close by and said, "Good morning, friends." Ned Christie "went by where Joe Eagle and Bear was and stopped near the hindmost man." Bear Grimmet got off his horse "to fix his stirrup leather," and suddenly the shooting erupted.[16]

Rat Panther corroborated Saddle Blanket's testimony that Eagle had done the shooting, while Pigeon stated that Eagle and Grimmet had each shot at the same time. Blair also testified that Eagle was the one who had done the shooting, as did Pigeon.[17]

Even so, when the preliminary hearing closed, the solicitor sought an indictment against Ned Christie, Eagle, and Lanaheate. This the court granted and adjourned until a future day to consider the evidence against Pigeon, Blair, and Taylor Christie, who were "claimed by the evidence to be complicated in the murder of Bare Grimmet."[18]

Guilty or not, Ned Christie was now in deeper trouble. The Cherokee Nation deputies would be after him as well as the federal deputies.

One evening he rode up the hollow in back of his cabin to the home of George Wilson, who lived a mile and a half north on Bitting Creek. He entered quietly and sat in a dignified manner as was the custom when visiting. After a respectful period he began to talk. He told Wilson he would like to buy his new .44 caliber Winchester. Wilson liked Ned and sold him the gun as requested. Ned, according to George's son, Eli, "was certainly glad to get the new gun and believed he would be able to live a little longer with his family by being able to kill a few more of those marshals."[19]

Ned Christie, the outlaw, with some of his favorite weapons. *Courtesy Northeastern State University, Tahlequah.*

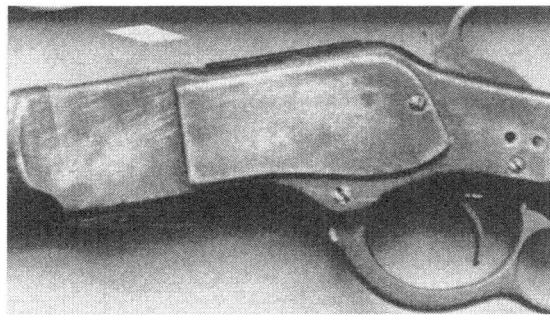

Christie's Winchester, now on display in the museum of the Fort Smith National Historic Site. Translated, these Cherokee words, "Nede Wade," engraved on the stock and plate, mean Ned Christie. *Photo by Bonnie Speer.*

71

CHAPTER 9

In the Fort Smith Court

It almost became a matter of habit. At the beginning of each federal court term in Fort Smith, the U.S. deputy marshals would drift into the marshal's office and come out armed with a new writ for Ned Christie's arrest. Then they would head toward Rabbit Trap, hoping to catch a glimpse of their elusive prey.

Meanwhile, John Parris and Charley Bobtail remained confined in the noisy, smelly federal jail, trying to catch the attention of a sympathetic ear at every opportunity. Finally, on March 7, 1888, each of them was released on $5,000 bond signed by friends and relatives. They were ordered to appear in court on the first day of the May term and from term to term thereafter until discharged by order of the court.[1]

Bub Trainor, the cause of everyone's trouble, appeared in court periodically in response to the various charges against him. On March 25, his case in the matter of the death of Deputy Maples was continued to the fall term. In May his attorney filed application for three witnesses: Nancy Shell, Will Dinsmore and Lucy Hicks. By them Trainor stated he could "prove that at the time and for some time before the killing he was at the residence of Nancy Shell eating supper, about 1/2 mile from the place of the killing, that he had been there for about two hours before the killing."[2] He pleaded guilty, during the May court term, to two counts of introducing and selling and was again committed to jail to await sentence.[3]

Then the Fort Smith court took its inevitable summer holiday when it ran out of funds again. Over 400 witnesses, "who had been compelled to come to the court, were dismissed." Some of them had been there four weeks and "many were without the means of getting home." All criminal cases were continued to the August term.[4]

When the court reconvened in August, the grand jury found 195 true bills of indictment and ignored 65, including Bub Trainor's assault case against Jackson Ellis and one charge for introducing and selling in 1886. Following this event, Trainor was released from jail with orders to appear on September 17 to stand trial for the murder of Maples. But he did not show up and was arrested again ten days later.

Trainor's arson trial was still pending. Conviction of arson carried a penalty of two to twenty-one years at hard labor. On October 1, Trainor made application for the following witnesses: Dave Williams, Joe Williams, George Mitchell of Oaks; Henry Chambers, Claremore; and Bob Rose, Tahlequah.[5]

Trainor stated that by witness George Mitchell he could prove that "long before the burning alleged in the indictment against him taht [sic] the prosecuting witness, Duckworth, told witness that he had sold out his entire interest in the business and everything pertaining thereto to William Israel, a Cherokee citizen."

By Henry Chambers, former treasurer of the Cherokee Nation, Trainor said he could prove that Israel had paid all the taxes on the store house before it was burned, and by Bob Rose, the current treasurer, he could prove essentially the same.

Trainor stated that by Dave and Joe Williams he could prove that on the night of the alleged arson, he was at the house of Dave Williams, asleep with Joe

Williams and that he did not leave the place until the next morning.

All the witnesses lived at or near the places indicated in the Cherokee Nation. Because Trainor said he did not possess sufficient means to pay the fees and expenses of the witnesses to testify in his behalf, he asked that they be summoned at the expense of the court.

The murder case of his father, Thomas W. Trainor, came to trial the first week of October. John Hawkins, the late high sheriff in the Cherokee Nation, and his deputy Sam Manus were acquitted by the jury. The verdict was "nothing more than expected by those familiar with the case," stated the Muskogee *Indian Arrow*.[6] Bub Trainor was admitted to bail again on December 31. The young outlaw's bond was signed by an imposing group of prominent men in the Cherokee Nation: Joel B. Mayes, Clem V. Rogers (father of Will Rogers), Lucien B. Bell, Elias C. Boudinot, Richard F. Boudinot, John H. Coody, and Jesse B. Mayes. Each guaranteed bond for Trainor in the amount of $1,000 for arson and assault with intent to kill, $5,000 for murder, and $500 for introducing and selling. Trainor was ordered to appear for the February term.[7]

Shortly after his release from jail, a seemingly strange thing occurred: Trainor was hired as a U.S. deputy marshal by the Fort Smith court. But it was not such an uncommon thing as one might presume, for it was an odd quirk of Judge Parker's that the character of many of his deputies could not bear close scrutiny. None of them were angels and many were bullies. Nearly all were said to be "coarse talking and unsentimental individuals," for Parker often hired known outlaws to hunt other outlaws. He excused this practice by stating that he was "obliged to take such material for deputies as proved efficient in serving the process of this court" for a man could "be highly moral but he did not have what it took to be a marshal in the Indian Country."[8]

Parker's idiosyncrasy and the hiring of Bub Trainor were soon to have a disastrous effect on the life of Ned Christie.

CHAPTER 10

Shot!

The federal court of the Western District of Arkansas had a new marshal. Jacob Yoes took over from Marshal Carroll on May 28, 1889, after being appointed by President Benjamin Harrison shortly after he took office in January. A husky individual with a blunt looking face and dark hair, Yoes was a man of strong will and temperament, which did not always sit well with those who worked with him.[1] Nevertheless, he felt fully competent in assuming the job.

At the time, many changes were taking place in Indian Territory. The Oklahoma Bill had passed in Congress, opening the Unassigned Lands to white settlement on April 22. In addition, the United States had established a civil court at Muskogee. With this encroachment of power in the Indian country, all knew it would be only a matter of time before the Five Civilized Tribes ceased to exist as individual nations and a way of life would be no more.

With white settlement in the Indian lands and the extension of the railroads, the bad people came with the good, to hide out in the rugged terrain and to terrorize whites and Indians alike. To quell this disruption Jacob Yoes meant to apply the law to the fullest and make the land safe for all.

In his first action, Marshal Yoes called in all the deputies and recommissioned those he wished to retain and replaced the others. Next he set about instituting new policies and cleaning up the backlog of business.[2]

Of particular concern to him was the long pending case of "Charley Bobtail *et al.*" Yoes agreed with Judge Parker that it was unthinkable to allow such a crime as the killing of a U.S. deputy marshal to go unpunished, but the case could not go to trial until Ned Christie was brought in.

Rumors about Christie had been pouring in, following the shooting of Bear Grimmet. On January 25, 1889, the *Fort Smith Elevator* reported "another killing on the Caney at the residence of Jess Pigeon, with Ned Christie and Pigeon doing the bloody work."[3] Two months later the paper stated that Ned Christie, "a Cherokee desperado and outlaw," had been killed or wounded by Zeke Proctor and "one England."[4]

"Well, if Ned has been 'monkeying' around with Zeke Proctor," the paper commented a week later, "it would not surprise us if the rumor was correct."[5]

Proctor, a Cherokee citizen, had gained notoriety following the accidental shooting of a woman at the Beck mill in the Flint District during a fight in 1872. During the subsequent trial in Indian court, a U.S. posse tried to arrest Proctor. Another fight erupted leaving ten dead, and Proctor escaped. After this event it seemed that every outrage in Indian Territory was blamed on him. Rumors held that he had killed twenty-three men. At last the United States granted Proctor amnesty and he settled down to become a law-abiding citizen again, winning much admiration from those who knew him.

Like Proctor, now it seemed every crime in Indian country was being blamed on Christie. Few of the deputy marshals were anxious to come up against him, but occasionally one tried. They soon learned that Christie's usual trick was to quit firing for a while; then when the deputies thought he was dead, and moved toward the house, Christie would open up on them again.

Yet, Christie must be brought in, Yoes determined, if the Maples murder case was ever to be brought to trial. One day in August, he summoned his most able deputy marshal, Heck Thomas, who had just brought in a wagonload of prisoners.[6] Handing him a writ for Christie, he reminded Thomas there was a standing reward of $500 for the Cherokee outlaw which would make his arrest worthwhile. In addition, he gave him another handful of writs and subpoenas.

As a rule Thomas liked to manhunt alone, or with just one or two trusted posse men. This time, he chose L.P. Isbell of Vinita. Isbell was a level-headed, cautious sort, a skilled tracker, almost as good with a gun as Heck.

The two started on the usual circuit through Indian Territory, handing out subpoenas and making arrests. By the time they reached Muskogee, they had thirteen prisoners. Leaving them under guard at Evans Stable, they met Bub Trainor.[7] Trainor knew the Going Snake District well. He also knew Ned Christie and his habits. That Trainor was accused in the same murder case did not seem to matter; or perhaps, like the officers of the Fort Smith court, Heck Thomas was also convinced that Ned Christie was the guilty party.

The three law officers set out on Christie's trail. After three weeks of tracking him, they located him at his home in Rabbit Trap. Heck Thomas sought the assistance of U.S. Deputy Marshals Rusk and Salmon in capturing the wily outlaw.[8]

The five deputies arrived in the vicinity of Christie's home before dawn on Thursday, September 26. Thomas planned to surround the house quietly, then wait for daylight, and for Christie to come out.[9]

Inside the house, Christie slept on, unaware of the deputies creeping through the trees. The constant pressure on him had begun to tell, and the deputy marshals were a constant menace to his family.

Between raids by the law officers, Christie tried to make his living peaceably in his blacksmith shop. But the deputies would not leave him alone, and he had to rely on his friends to warn him, or else barricade himself in his home. As his reputation had grown the sympathy of those in the Keetoowah had lessened. Christie slept with his Winchester and kept an ample supply of ammunition at hand. But all of this had become wearisome and at the urging of his good friend, Amos Crittenden, he had about decided to surrender.[10]

Recently he had discussed his situation with W. L. "Tuxie" Miller, his twenty-six-year-old neighbor, who lived a half-mile north. "Tux, if I knew I could get a fair trial," Christie told him, " I would give myself up."[11]

But now as the grey light of dawn crept across the land, the dogs in the yard began to bark, and Christie sprang up, his Winchester in hand.

Outside the house, Heck Thomas made a quick change in plans. He signaled for the deputies to rush the cabin. When they got up to it, they could hear someone inside "crawling to the loft."[12] Thomas shouted, "United States marshals!" and demanded that Christie surrender.[13]

Christie did not answer. Instead, he knocked a plank off the gabled end of the cabin, gobbled at the deputies, and opened fire. The deputies returned a hail of bullets. Again Thomas demanded Christie's surrender. Once more Christie refused. Thomas warned him if he was going to fight to send out his women and children, that the deputies were going to set his house afire.[14]

Christie cracked down on the lawmen with the loud Winchester. Thomas "then fired a small out-building* near the house," hoping to smoke him out, and all the

---

*Some sources indicate this was a smokehouse, others state it was Christie's gunshop.

men took positions behind trees "to await developments." A woman ran out of the house. The officers held their fire until she had escaped in the direction of the spring.[15]

The shooting began again. Heck Thomas and Isbell positioned themselves behind the same tree. In turning around, Isbell exposed his left shoulder and received a Winchester ball through it, shattering the bones badly.[16]

The flames from the out-building had now taken hold of the cabin. Smoke billowed from under the eaves. The deputies waited for Christie to come out. In the early morning light, they saw a figure dash forth. Thinking it was Christie, Thomas shouted for him to "hold up." But it was not Christie, it was the boy. He tried to climb over the fence and the deputies fired, striking him three times. He fell, but managed to escape in the tall weeds.[17]

By now Isbell was "becoming very faint and sick." Believing that Christie had escaped and fearing the woman, who had run out, might bring reinforcements, the deputy marshals retired to where they had left their horses. From there they made their way to a place of safety.[18]

Behind them, in the loft of the burning house, unknown to the lawmen, Ned Christie lay wounded, unable to move.

U.S. Deputy Marshal Heck Thomas, shot Ned Christie, destroying the sight in his left eye, and burned his home, leading Christie to vow he would never give up. *Courtesy Beth Thomas Meeks.*

U.S. Marshal Jacob Yoes who made an all out effort to capture Ned Christie. *Courtesy Fort Smith National Historic Site.*

81

CHAPTER 11

A Vindictive Hatred

How long Ned Christie lay helpless in the loft of the burning cabin it is impossible to know. Early in the fight he had been peeking through the hole in the end of the gable when one of the deputy marshals scored a direct hit. The bullet smashed Christie's nose, struck his left eye, ranged around the side of his head, and lodged in the back just beneath the skin.[1]

When this happened, he "turned blind and fell, right on his back on the floor of the upstairs." Fully conscious, he could not move, see, or speak. He could hear the officers outside the house and "the thing that worried him most, he was afraid they would notice that he had quit shooting. Then they would come rushing in and pick him up while he was unable to speak."[2]

Christie heard his son[*] grab his Winchester and start firing through the opening in the gable. He "kept firing often enough to keep them believing he was up yet and that perhaps he was playing his usual trick on them." While his son stalled the deputies, Ned began to see "a spot of light before him, about the size of a pin head." The spot grew larger and larger. After awhile Ned could see everything. His mind had been "perfectly clear," the whole time. He still could neither move nor talk. Then his son "shot one of the posse," and the house

---

[*]The identity of this boy has provided some confusion for historians. Eli Wilson (Indian-Pioneer Papers, vol. 99, p. 142), the source of information about this incident, stated that the boy was Ned's son, Arch Christie. However, legal records show that

caught fire. Since the boy could not move his father, he decided to leave the cabin.

Christie heard the sound of gunshots outside as his son tried to escape. The lawmen left. Smoke swirled into the loft and flames crackled below. Shortly afterwards Christie heard someone calling his name in Cherokee.[3] His wife had returned as soon as the lawmen withdrew, and finding the place apparently deserted and the cabin on fire she ran inside, searching for him. In a moment, she reached the opening at the top of the ladder, and her frightened eyes saw him lying upstairs, wounded and seemingly unconscious.[4]

Other relatives and friends living nearby came running to see what the shooting was about. Together they managed to get Ned downstairs out of the house before it was consumed by the flames, and took him to the hills.[5]

In the woods they found his son shot in the back. One bullet had glanced "across the back, the other passing from back to front through the right lung." The boy seemed near death, and Christie was also badly wounded. The Indians sent for Dr. Bitting at the mill.[6]

Meanwhile, the deputy marshals rode toward Tahlequah. They were "seven hours on the road, Isbell being too sick to move rapidly."[7] Their arrival in town caused considerable excitement. Much concern was expressed for the wounded deputy. Heck Thomas

---

Arch Christie, also known as Arch Wolf and "Little Arch,"was not Ned's son but that of his sister, Betsy Christie Wolf, and Jack Wolf. Ned Christie had only one legal son, James. Contemporary newspaper accounts of the fight do not give the boy's name but simply state he was Christie's son. James Christie, according to census records, was twelve years old at the time of the shooting, which agrees with the age reported later in the newspaper. Also Heck Thomas noted in his daybook in regard to the fight, "N.C.-Betsy Wolf. Jack Christy [Ned's brother] knows age of boy....Has 3 children 2 girls and boy....

"installed Isbell in the Hotel Deflouarney where physicians Fite and Treadwell tended to his wound."[8]

Following this action, Thomas telegraphed Marshal Yoes about their ill-fated attempt to arrest Ned Christie. Yoes issued a new writ for Christie, charging him with resisting arrest with intent to kill.[9]

The *Tahlequah Telephone* reported that "Christie and his boy—a lad of 12 years—are both fatally wounded, and the boy is not expected to live but a short time."[10]

After leaving Isbell in the care of the doctors, Heck Thomas returned to Rabbit Trap with his posse on Saturday. They scoured the community and found the injured boy. They also learned that Ned Christie had been "wounded in the forehead but had escaped from the burning house after the officers left and was hid in the woods."[11]

Considerable animosity toward the deputies existed in the neighborhood because of the incident. Even so, the lawmen continued searching for Christie. Tuxie Miller recalled the event:

That same night the officers came to our house and demanded supper and their horses fed. We lived one-half mile from Christie and about one and one-half from his father. When Ft. Smith officers were out rounding up outlaws they always did that. People had to do as they ordered. They'd always pay. Heck Thomas, one of the marshals, was the one who ordered supper. There were five of them.

The officers offered me a Winchester and 100 rounds of cartridges if I'd go over to Ned's house and find out if he was dead or alive. They must have suspected that some of his folks had gone back in the house to see whether he was killed or not.

I went over to Ned's father and says, "Where's Ned?"

He says, "Down in the ravine."

I asked him if he was dead, and he said no.

I went back then to the officers, but I didn't tell them where Ned was. They asked me if he was dead or alive, and I told them that I couldn't find out. Never did get the Winchester or the shells.[12]

Next morning the deputy marshals returned to Tahlequah. They found Isbell improved, and, though his wound was not considered necessarily dangerous, it was believed it would "probably make him a cripple for life."[13]

Rumors persisted that Christie had died. The *Muskogee Phoenix* reported, "Marshal Thomas who gave us the particulars of the shooting, says that Christie is known to have killed eight men in his time, four of whom have been killed since the shooting of Marshal Maples.[14]

The *Tahlequah Telephone* noted that Heck Thomas was expected to remain in Tahlequah with Isbell for "several days before he could remove him safely as Christie has five brothers and other relatives who may make trouble with them."[15]

Then the "latest from the Caney" came, claiming that Christie was "but slightly injured and is now up going about his business."[16]

The *Telephone* expressed its doubt: "...this story is not to be regarded as authentic for it does not corroborate with more reliable information received from Dr. Biddings [sic] the physician who attended Christie after that trouble. We are also reliably informed that with proper attention the boy will recover."[17]

The *Telephone* reviewed the story of Christie in depth, relating in part:

Almost 25 [sic] east of this place is the home of Ned Christie, an outlaw, who has since the fall of 1886 [sic] made for himself a name that to hear mentioned, made the average Deputy Marshal and officer of the law tremble with fear.

In the latter part of 1886 [sic] a Deputy United States Marshal named Maples, was shot from ambush in the upper part of this town, and circumstances made Christie an alleged accomplice to the crime.

The charge, whether false or true, made Ned Christie an outlaw, for he, like many of his race, looked upon the U.S. Court and "Aunt Delilah" with a sense of awe and thought it almost certain death to be arraigned before the Fort Smith tribunal under such a charge.

Let that be as it may, Christie has distinguished himself since as a most fearless and dangerous outlaw, and while he possessed many warm friends in the nation, he has been the cause of much anxiety and fear on the part of others.

At the time of the Maples killing Christie was a member of the Executive Council of the Cherokee Nation and was considered a good, peaceable citizen, and in this instance it is to be more fully realized and lamented that circumstances too often shape a man's destiny.

...The marshals express their regrets for having to burn Christie's house, but it was entirely necessary in order to get him out. Christie was also to blame for the boy being shot, for the marshals say they entreated him to send his family from the house, as they intended to have him, regardless of circumstances.[18]

After several days, seeing he could do nothing else for Isbell and being advised it was best to not move him yet, Heck Thomas left Isbell at Tahlequah. He gathered his prisoners at Muskogee, and with his posse, headed for Fort Smith.[19] There he reported to Marshal Yoes that Ned Christie was up and around, "not withstanding his wound in the forehead," and the boy who was shot was recovering.[20]

In Rabbit Trap, though Christie was not critically wounded, Dr. Bitting considered his injury a serious matter. The bullet had smashed the bridge of Christie's nose, ruining his good looks, and put out the sight in his left eye.

A few days after the shooting, some of Christie's young friends, asked him about the fight. Christie told them how the bullet had entered his head and he had fallen on the floor, and how his son had shot back at the marshals. The listeners marveled at the missile that could still be felt in the back of Christie's head, "rolling inside the skin."[21]

John Henry Pedford, twenty-one, asked if the shot was not very painful. Ned replied, "No, like a bee sting."[22]

But a vindictive hatred now burned in his heart. His son had been shot, his home destroyed, his face disfigured, and the sight in his left eye lost, all for a crime he had not committed.

According to the *Daily Oklahoman*:

Christie now swore that never would he surrender, nor would he ever be taken alive. At the same time he stated that he bore the officer [sic] no enmity personally but would shoot whenever they came within range of his gun. There was only one man in the whole world he said whom he would like to shoot, and that was Bud [sic] Trainor, who was doing all he could to assist the officers to capture or kill Christie. But he never got within range of Christie's Winchester rifle.[23]

CHAPTER 12

Here He Would Die

The deputy marshals continued their pursuit of Ned Christie and as he considered his vulnerable position, his mind must have wandered back to ancient times. During those days, the Cherokees had been warlike and built walled forts for protection. These forts were located beside running water, with a lookout tree and a posted guard. Why not a similar fort for himself?

With his friends and relatives, Christie selected a site on a hilltop a half-mile west of his burned cabin. From here he could view the entire valley along Bitting Creek. Water was available from a spring which flowed out of the rocks at the foot of the hill. The main road from Sallisaw to Tahlequah wound around the base of the hill so that anyone moving along the road could not pass without being detected. On the hilltop, the Indians erected a wooden shelter with a rock wall around it. They stocked the fort with food, water, and ammunition.* As a final precaution they cleared the trees from the top of the hill, making "Ned's Mountain" virtually impregnable.[1]

Feeling secure in the rock fort with his guards, Christie sent word to Deputy Marshal Thomas as to where he could be found, informing the officer that if he thought he could capture him to come and they would shoot it out.[2] But Thomas did not reply.

---

*The remains of Ned Christie's stone fort can still be seen on top of Ned's Mountain.

During the next few weeks, Christie and his son improved steadily. Dr. Bitting was skilled in the use of Indian medicines as well as that of the white man. In addition, Ned's brother Goback was one of the most respected herb doctors around.

Many of the remedies used by Indian doctors in those days were held as profound secrets. Some knew how to make a wax from certain roots that could draw the infection out of a gunshot wound, thus preventing infection.[3] Faith healers knew many chants and rituals that could be used in curing the sick. Reportedly, Nancy Jumper could stop a fever by placing a live coal in water, uttering some Cherokee words over it, then asking the patient to sip the water, and blowing four times upon him.[4]

By the first of November, Christie's son was well enough that the *Fort Smith Elevator* could report, "Though attended by only an 'Ingin' doctor, the little fellow is recovering, and is able to hobble around."[5]

Meanwhile, Heck Thomas was making plans for an assault on the rock fort. During the first week of November, after spending a month in Fort Smith settling his accounts, visiting his family, and testifying in various court cases, he began organizing his posse. He left Fort Smith on November 6 with Bub Trainor, James Farr, and Britt Simmons at his side.[6] Along the way, he picked up Joe Caudell, Sam Simmons, John McEachin, and James McNolly.[7]

The posse reached Rabbit Trap on November 12. There it found Christie entrenched in his rock fort, daring them to approach. The deputies conferred on the matter. Most of them believed "it would take a large regiment of U.S. militia to stand up to Christie and the powerful defense surrounding him."[8] Heck Thomas did not want to expose his men needlessly to the danger. He called off the assault and contented himself with scouring the neighborhood for information about

Christie and the boy, before leaving the community with his posse.[9]

This was Heck Thomas' final attempt to capture Ned Christie. He held a double commission, one in the Fort Smith court and a second in the new court established at Paris, Texas, in 1866. The Paris court oversaw the southern part of Indian Territory. In disagreement with some of Marshal Yoes' strict policies, Thomas soon rode out of the Tahlequah area and took a deputy's job in the Paris court. He established a home for his family at White Bead Hill in the Chickasaw Nation.[10] Evidently Trainor also moved to the Paris court, for on November 26, Thomas noted in his daybook that he had purchased a new gun and scabbard for Trainor.[11] However, their relationship ended abruptly on January 23, 1890, when deputy marshals Trainor and Robert Hutchins shot Jim Starr.

Jim Starr, alias Jim July, was a nephew of July Perryman of the Creek Nation, "and sort of an adopted son to old Tom Starr," who called him Jim July Starr.[12] Shortly after Belle Starr's husband, Bill Starr, and Jim West killed each other in a fight, Belle had invited Jim Starr to move into the cabin with her at Younger's Bend. The pair openly let it be known they were living together as man and wife to protect Belle's claim to her property there, as the Choctaw Nation was trying to oust her as an intruder, following Bill Starr's death.[13] Charged with horse stealing in 1887, Jim Starr was out of jail on bond. He had given appearance regularly at each court term in Fort Smith, until Belle was murdered by an unknown assailant on February 2, 1889.

On that morning, Starr had been on his way to Fort Smith to appear before the court again, and Belle accompanied him part way. On her return home, somebody murdered her with a shotgun. When the news reached Starr, he left town immediately, promising revenge.[14]

Following Belle's funeral, Starr accused a tenant farmer, Edgar A. Watson, of the crime. Making a citizen's arrest, he took him to Fort Smith where Watson appeared before the grand jury. But he was released for lack of evidence. Disgusted with the turn of events, Starr jumped bail and went on the scout.[15]

Meanwhile Deputy Marshal Bob Hutchins obtained information which he believed indicated that Starr himself had killed his wife and tried to frame Watson. On hearing that Starr was headed for the Chickasaw country, Hutchins, with Bub Trainor, set out after him. Coming upon him near Ardmore, the two men hid in a thicket and shot Starr's horse from under him and mortally wounded him. Heck Thomas brought the unfortunate man to Fort Smith with a load of prisoners on the train.[16] Starr told the officers that if he died to have Trainor and Hutchins tried for murder as "they shot me foul."[17]

The following day as he lay suffering in the jail hospital, Starr told a reporter from the *Fort Smith Elevator* that Trainor and Hutchins had waylaid him nine miles from Ardmore and fired on him without warning.[18] When the reporter asked if he had not been running from them when they shot him, Starr replied that he had not run until after he was wounded, and that they then shot his horse three times, killing the animal. Starr lingered for several days, in much pain. Following his death, he was buried in Potter's Field.[19]

Trainor and Hutchins were each charged with Starr's murder and arrested.* A week later, David

---

*Bob Hutchins died on April 29, 1951. In his biography, *Gunman's Territory*, written by Elmer LeRoy Baker, Hutchins claimed sole responsibility for shooting Starr. He said Trainor had been drinking, and was passed out on the ground.[20]

Trainor arrived in Fort Smith to "help his brother Bub get up bond."[21] By now Heck Thomas seemingly had enough of the wild, young man—or perhaps it was Judge Parker who made the final decision. At any rate, on his release on bond, Bub Trainor left the marshal's force and returned to his old outlaw gang.

In Rabbit Trap, Ned Christie continued to improve until he felt he was "able to be up and do some more fighting."[22] He returned to the site of his burned cabin. Most Cherokees had a deep love for their simple homes, and it can be assumed that Ned Christie was no different. Now he determined to rebuild his cabin, making it a permanent fort which would provide maximum security.

He chose a new location, a steep slope directly across Bitting Creek and 150 yards above the spring. Here with the help of friends and relatives, Christie rapidly erected his new home.

When it was finished, the twenty-by-twenty-foot building stood two stories high and was securely grounded on a sandstone foundation.[23] It had double log walls for extra protection. (Some claim sand was poured between the walls.) A root cellar was located beneath the cabin. The structure had a minimum of openings, following the pattern of early Cherokee homes, and only a single door faced the creek. In the upper story on every side, Christie cut "portholes," about ten inches square. From these openings, he could keep watch for his enemies and fire on them as they approached.[24]

He cleared a field of fire around the cabin, cutting down the big trees which encircled it. He located his out-buildings far enough from the cabin that the disastrous episode of the smokehouse (or gun shop) could not be repeated. James Padgett, his brother-in-law, helped him build a split rail fence around the clearing.[25]

Christie fortified his new home with a small arsenal and much ammunition. Then with a few simple necessities and plenty of food and water, he and his family set up housekeeping again. Here, he vowed, he would stay and fight to the death before he would let the deputies take him alive.[26]

CHAPTER 13

Too Violent to Condone

Judge Parker was a constant thorn in the side of the deputies sent out to capture Ned Christie. He found it irritating that a single Indian could outwit all the skilled trackers and crack marksmen of the United States marshal's force.

Some of the failure of the deputy marshals in bringing in the "Wolf of the Cookson Hills" was attributed to the stiff regulations laid down by the ruling powers in Washington. The department's system of fees was such that it did not make it financially feasible to take the risk of hunting such dangerous game as Ned Christie.

W.E. Hazen, Examiner of the Western District of Arkansas, addressed this problem in his annual report of March 1890 to the Justice Department in which he stated:

> ...under the regulations here Deputies are considered to be employed to *make arrests* not to serve in *endeavoring* to do so. In some cases repeated unsuccessful endeavors to effect arrests have cost the Deputies largely more than their entire fees when arrests were finally accomplished.[1]

Hazen cited the case of Ned Christie, "a notorious Indian murderer and outlaw," as a striking illustration. He wrote that after a three-week hunt by deputies,

Isbell had been wounded so as to undoubtedly cripple him for life. For this Isbell could receive no pay under the rigid rules in force. The danger incurred and the wound received were simply parts of an unsuccessful endeavor to arrest.

Hazen added that this was but one case among many. He believed that in well-authenticated cases of this kind exceptions could be made by the U.S. District Attorney without opening the way for fraud through charges for expenses incurred in fictitious endeavors. He also noted that in many instances the expenses made in endeavoring were as clearly apparent as the fees chargeable when a prisoner was actually brought in. Hazen and the other officers in the Fort Smith court were well aware that until something was done to provide greater incentive for the deputies to try to arrest Ned Christie nothing was going to be done.

In Rabbit Trap, Christie was enjoying a time of comparative peace, sheltered within the thick log walls of his new home. His son had recovered from his wounds. The Cherokee Census Rolls of 1890 provides evidence that Mary, Ned's eldest daughter, 16, had moved in with the family.[*2] She brought along her one-year-old daughter Charlotte, fathered by George Gritts.[3] In all likelihood Ned Christie delighted in having his family around him, for the Cherokees had always regarded their children fondly, and Ned, in particular, seemed to enjoy having young people around. He had a special following among those in the neighborhood. They regarded him as something of a hero, what with his strong physique, his intelligence, and his boldness in battle against deputy marshals. They believed he fought only to protect his own life and to preserve his home.

---

*This refutes several stories which claimed that the two women living in the house were both wives of Ned Christie.

Among those with whom Christie had established an especially close relationship was his nephew, Arch Wolf, now fourteen-years-old. Arch, born in 1876, the same year as Ned's own son, James, was the son of Jack Wolf of the Going Snake District and Ned's sister, Betsy Christie Wolf Young of the Flint District.[4] Sometimes Arch Wolf was called "Arch Christie," because he was the grandson of Watt Christie's brother, Arch Christie. To avoid confusion the family habitually called the older Arch "Big Arch," and the younger one "Little Arch."[5] Little Arch's Indian name was "Walk About."[6]

Little Arch stood fairly short and wore the rough spun jacket and trousers of the white man. He was round of face with dark and brooding eyes. Ned Christie liked Little Arch and took him into his home.

During that summer of 1890, Ned Christie's reputation as an outlaw continued to grow. Every store robbery and other depredation in the area was blamed on him, though a number of other outlaw gangs operated in the vicinity.

In one such instance, Christie supposedly robbed Levi Keys' store at Wauhillau "two or three times." The first night, Keys was visiting Tom Duckworth, who lived nearby. The two men heard chopping in the direction of the store. Fearing robbers were breaking the door down, the men grabbed guns. They believed it was Ned Christie and his gang. Duckworth wanted to shoot Christie, but Keys said no. They found nothing when they arrived.[7]

In another instance, Lucinda Sanders Wilhite, who grew up in Wauhillau, stated that Christie asked to hide in the loft of Keys' store as U.S. deputy marshals were searching for him nearby. Keys refused his request, fearing for his own safety. Shortly after this incident, it was supposedly U.S. deputies who wanted to use the store as a hideout while searching for Christie, but again Keys said no, for if the outlaws found out about his involvement with the law, they would kill him.[8]

Catherine Wilhite, a relative of Lucinda's who also lived at Wauhillau, related a similar story:

Ned Christie come here and robbed my uncle's (Keys) store...at Old Wauhillau...he took an axe and chopped down the door. When Christie heard the marshal coming he would go down by Hungry Mountain.

One night when I was a little kid, somebody knocked on the door and Momma says, "Who is it?" "The U.S. marshals." She thought it was Pap. "Jim, get up and let the U.S. marshals in." When opened the door, whole slew came in. Kicked up the fire and made a light. Hunting Ned Christie. Thought they had seen him about Old Sully Eagle's down there. But Momma told them no, nobody was down there at Old Sully Eagle's that she knew. There was respect for women and children then.[9]

Once a woman accused Christie of stealing a horse. The charge was formally pressed in Indian court but the woman did not appear and the charge was dismissed.[10]

It was rumored that Ned had taken to selling bootleg whiskey to help support his family.* The story is told that one day at the depot, where he had gone to pick up his personal supply, which he had ordered delivered there, Christie entertained the folks by firing

---

*If this was true no legal charges of it can be found in the National Archives. Records from the Fort Smith court, however, do show that Arch Wolf was charged with two counts of introducing and selling.[11]

from the hip at the glass insulators on the telegraph poles.[12]

On October 31, the *Fort Smith Elevator* reported:

> Ned Christie, the Cherokee outlaw, and two brothers named Squirrel, were engaged in a little game of draw near the home of Christie. They got into a fight and Christie was cut severely, once in the shoulder and twice in the head. One of the Squirrels was shot by Christie.[13]

A week later, the *Elevator* further remarked:

> It will be remembered that a little over a year ago the house of Christie was burned by deputy marshals in an attempt to capture him. It is said he had rebuilt in the middle of his field, the house being a double-log structure with port holes on every side. No one can approach in the day time without being seen and he keeps eight or ten dogs who raise a furious alarm if any one approaches at night.[14]

As Christie's reputation continued to grow, the support of his former friends dropped away. Though they did not turn him in, many now felt that his criminal activities were becoming too violent to condone.

In Fort Smith, those officials in the federal court agreed. Soon an official document dated October 15, arrived from Washington authorizing U.S. Marshal Jacob Yoes to offer a $1,000 reward for the arrest and delivery of "one Ned Christie at the Jail in Fort Smith; the said Christie having been indicted in this court for the murder of U.S. Deputy Daniel Maples."[15]

The reward was established five days later, and Marshal Yoes and Judge Parker sat back, confident that it would be only a matter of time until the troublesome Cherokee outlaw would be brought in.

CHAPTER 14

The Hunt Intensifies

Activity picked up among the deputies as news spread of the $1,000 reward for Ned Christie, for that amount was equivalent to a year's pay for the law officers at regular wages. Lawmen roamed the woods in the Going Snake District, hunting Christie "like a rabbit." Often he was "jumped up" and shot it out with the deputies.[1]

One day Christie escaped into a dense thicket. The pursuing officers were certain they had him this time. They paused at the edge of the brush, arguing who would go in to flush out their dangerous prey. Then they heard Christie's defiant gobble on the other side of the thicket and knew he was out and laughing at them.[2]

Eli Wilson, a neighbor of Ned's, remembered in 1937:

...They [the officers] always tried to slip up on him and kill him while he was about his work around the little farm.

The mystery of all this slipping up business was, they always failed to slip up on him. He had very wise and reliable Indian fortune tellers at his command, and he always told his family to leave the house about an hour before the marshals were to be there. He and his son, Arch, ate their meal the last thing, and brought in plenty of drinking water. Then they examined their guns and put the ammunition in pouches

100

and hung them on their persons. Then they put their guns in the portholes ready for action.[3]

When a battle occurred, Wilson and the others in the neighborhood could hear the sounds ringing through the valley. When the shooting stopped, they knew the deputy marshals had left. Then Wilson said he and his brothers would:

go running down there to see the battle ground and pick up empty cartridge shells, and to see how many men Ned had killed or wounded...by the time we got down there Ned would be outside looking about the place, seeing what needed to be done. He would see if the cows needed to be milked, or the horses needed to be watered. After he finished his chores, he would play marbles with us boys with a great deal of delight and often laughed very heartily. A lot of his neighbors always came to visit him and to express their joy that he had come through safe once more. You see, Ned was a nice neighbor, and a very intelligent man to talk with...Ned said he always just had to shoot one or two and the rest always made that an excuse to leave, to carry their wounded back to town for medical attention. He said he would peep through some hole in his log house and watch them loading the injured men into wagons to haul them away. He said nearly every time they got so careless about staying behind trees he could have killed two or three more of them easily. He always felt sorry for those men and just contented himself by letting them go back home once more to see their wives and children...Very few people ever knew that his son, Arch Christie, always stayed hid in the house, so as to be ready to help his father fight when the U.S. Marshals came again.[4]

Deputy Marshal Milo Creekmore seemed particularly eager to capture Ned Christie. Creekmore joined Marshal Jacob Yoes' force in the spring of 1890.[5] His brother Rudolph B. Creekmore was also a deputy marshal.[6]

William Hugh Winder operated a small sawmill in Rabbit Trap, about a half-mile from Christie. One day Creekmore, a good shot, bragged to Winder and his hired hand, Alex Holt, that he was going to get Ned Christie. The word reached Christie, who sent his brother-in-law, Sam Manus, up the valley to see Winder, who lived a half-mile from Christie. Manus informed Winder that Christie wanted him to come down to Daniel Gritts' place right away. In 1937 Winder related:

> I said to my wife, "Well, I guess I had better go, hadn't I?"
>
> "Why, Hugh, he may be just wanting to kill you."
>
> "Why no," I said. "I haven't done him any harm. Ned is my friend."
>
> So I went down. Ned jumped up and shook my hand. He seemed glad to see me. He said, "Mr. Winder, I hear a new United States Marshal has been appointed at Muskogee and he has promised the Government that he will catch me. Now, Mr. Winder, please get him word that I don't want to hurt him, but he better stay out of these woods and stay with his loving wife and children. And I also wanted to tell you that I am coming up to your sawmill and kill Alex Holt for talking too much and snitching on me to the United States marshals."
>
> I said, "Ned, I am not your enemy, not in any sense of the word and you know I never have and never will meddle in your business, but on account of this fellow Holt being at my saw mill I

want to beg you to please let him go and I will get him to leave tomorrow if I can, but give me a few days to get him out of the country, besides you will scare my wife to death if you do that."

He said, "Mr. Winder, on account of your pleas and for your wife's sake, I'll give you a few days to get him gone, but about this new marshal, Mr. Creekmore, I intend to shoot at his head the first glimpse I get of him."

I said, "That's all right, Ned, I haven't a word to say against that, but I will tell him what you said if I get a chance."

I left him with a smile on his face; he seemed pleased with the interview.

I told Creekmore the news, but he scorned it and took no heed and only said, "Aw, I am not afraid of Old Ned." In about a week, Ned took a shot at a man from a distance and the bullet barely missed his head and that man ran into the woods and he never was heard of again in that country.

The U.S. Marshal knocked on my door one morning just before daylight and wanted to come in, so I let him in and he searched all through my place for Ned Christie and after he got through, I said, "Mr. Creekmore, I want you to sit down a minute, I want to talk to you."

I told him all that Ned had said and he got up and gave me the horse laugh and said, "Nonsense, I am after old Ned and aim to get him the first time I come upon him."

Now Creekmore was a tall, blond, curly-headed man and a very over-confident sort of fellow. About three days afterward, I heard some shooting down below in the hollow, I recognized Ned's big forty-four Winchester talking and the other guns were of lesser report, probably high-powered army caliber rifles. In about thirty minutes a couple of men came running in the yard and one of them was this tall blond curly-headed man.

"Now what happened?" I said.

Curly said, "We been fighting the real Ned Christie. My God! He shot our horses dead in their tracks and before we could find a real good place to hide to do our shooting, he had killed our horses. And look at these holes in my hat, in my pocket, and my ear sure is bleeding, isn't it? what seems to be left of it, and look at my partner, he is shot two or three times, I don't know how bad."

I said, "Come in here and let me wash your ear."

After I washed them up, I found his deputy had only several flesh wounds about the body and Curly the prettiest letter U cut out of the end of his ear you ever saw. Curly left the forests and never came back.[7]

U.S. Deputy Marshal Dave Rusk was another person, seemingly intent on capturing Ned Christie. He had been with Heck Thomas on that ill-fated attempt when Isbell was wounded. Rusk was a small, husky man about five-feet-four. He had fought in the Civil War as a captain in the Confederate Army, First Battalion, Missouri Cavalry.[8] An expert marksman, he traveled with Robinson Brothers Circus after the war as an exhibition shooter. Eventually he joined the U.S. deputy marshal force. Yoes knew him to be devoted to his duty and full of energy.

Rusk "organized a group of Cherokees who were not favorable toward Ned Christie." The posse surrounded Ned's Fort. Ned uttered his turkey gobble. His aim was "uncanny. In a matter of minutes, he had wounded four of the posse. It was evident by the number of shots, Ned had several confederates." Rusk took stock of his wounded and called off the fight.[9]

Later Rusk made a lone attempt to sneak up on Christie. He scouted the hill country around Christie's home. Twice he managed to sneak up close enough to get a view of the fort. Each time he was fired upon by the "uncanny marksman." The last shot left a bullet hole in Rusk's black Stetson.

A few days later Christie sent an Indian boy with a note, which displayed his sense of humor, to the *Cherokee Advocate*: "I thought I saw a big, black potatoe bug in my garden but it turned out to be the hat of that 'little marshal'—Dave Rusk."[10]

A third dedicated law officer, who also seemed determined to have Christie, was U.S. Deputy Marshal Heck Bruner of Siloam Springs, reportedly "one of the most competent, venturesome officers known." A quiet man with a fierce gaze, he habitually held a cigar clamped between his teeth. A formidable officer, he had been called in on every major manhunt in Indian Territory.[11]

One day Bruner teamed with Deputy Marshal Barney Connelly, who had helped investigate the murder of Deputy Dan Maples. Now Connelly lived in Vinita and was a highly respected officer who had arrested scores of violaters. He was said to be a man of extreme caution.[12]

With great patience Bruner and Connelly crept within view of Ned's Fort. They shouted for Ned to surrender, but their call brought no response from the house. The deputies fired a shot into the air as a warning that they would start pumping lead into the house. A thunderous barrage answered their signal, cutting leaves and twigs about their heads. Bruner and Connelly beat a hasty retreat.[13]

For a time it seemed Ned Christie might never be captured. A legend began to build in the hill country of the Cherokee Nation that he was invincible. As Christie's reputation grew, Judge Parker became more and more irritable, and continued to mount pressure on the marshal's office. Finally, Marshal Yoes determined to make an all-out effort to corral the slippery outlaw.

CHAPTER 15

Gathering of the Forces

Ned Christie must have often pondered how he had gotten into his present situation. Occasionally news about Bub Trainor drifted into Rabbit Trap. Trainor's helpful attorney, Elias C. Boudinot, had died, and Trainor was still on the run from three counts of introducing and selling.[1] John Parris also continued in and out of trouble. Sentenced to a year in the Arkansas penitentiary for illegal whiskey selling, he had returned to his old business as soon as he was released and promptly ended up before Judge Parker again.[2]

It had now been five and a half years since Ned Christie began running from the deputies because of his alleged murder of Deputy Marshal Dan Maples. Those closest to him said he had never asked much except to be left alone so he could make a living for his family. Even now most of his neighbors believed he sought only to defend himself and his home, but rumors persisted that he was involved in illegal activities.

A case in point, on September 18, 1892, David M. Moore, "a white man and not all Indian," reported to law officials that his store at Moore's Mill, Arkansas, had been robbed. U.S. deputy marshals, who investigated the robbery, listed among the stolen goods eight pairs of boots, fifty yards of calico, fifty yards of domestic, twenty dozen spools of thread, twenty yards of velvet, and twenty breast pins.[3]

The deputies reported that the items had been "feloniously stolen, taken and carried away by a certain ill-disposed person...unknown..." and charged that George Christie, Arch Wolf, Jack Wolf, Jackson Wolf, and Jim Christie "feloniously did buy, receive, have and conceal" the items.[4]

The five men were subsequently indicted by the November grand jury and were ordered to stand trial in the May 1893 term.* If the court suspicioned that Ned Christie was that "certain ill-disposed person" who had stolen the goods, evidently it had no proof for he was not mentioned by name in the warrant for arrest.

Nevertheless, the thought must have been in the mind of Marshal Yoes as he set about putting into action a plan to capture Christie. Summoning Deputy Marshal Dave Rusk, he told him to get Christie regardless of what it cost. Rusk, in turn, contacted deputy marshals Charley Copeland, Milo Creekmore, and David C. Dye.

Copeland, from Siloam Springs, Arkansas, was a handsome, athletically built six-footer. His jovial personality made him a popular figure at social functions. He manifested raw courage when on a manhunt.[5] Creekmore was a different sort. After his attempt to arrest Christie, he had run afoul of the law himself the previous spring for unlawfully removing and concealing eight pints of whiskey from a warehouse in Eastland County, Texas. He was subsequently arrested and confined to jail for a time.[6]

Now free, Creekmore was back in the marshal's service and rode with Copeland and Dye toward Christie's home again, early on the morning of October 12, 1892. Along the way they picked up three assistants, including Joe Bowers and John Fields.[7]

---

*Jack Wolf and Jackson Wolf, half-brothers, were arrested on this charge that spring by Dave Rusk, but their case was dismissed for lack of evidence.[8]

Little is known of Bowers, but Fields was a half-blood Cherokee who reportedly "had the reputation of being one of the worst guns in that part of the territory," with a "habit of getting a few drinks under his belt and shooting up the town and running his horse into the business places, running everyone out."[9]

The posse reached Christie's house at dawn. In the pale light, they could see the cleared area which surrounded the two-story cabin. A wagon stood near the rail fence on one side. As the deputies closed in on the cabin, the dogs began to bark, and Rusk called out for Christie to surrender. The only answer was a volley of bullets, one of which hit Fields in the neck, inflicting a mortal wound. Another struck Bowers, disabling him.[10]

When it was found that Christie would not surrender, the officers warned the women and children to come out, which they did, and were placed under guard.

The deputy marshals then set fire to the outbuildings, hoping the flames would ignite the house as before. When this attempt failed, the deputies tried dynamite, but the fuse refused to burn.

Creekmore rode hurriedly to Tahlequah. He sent a telegram to Marshal Yoes which appeared in the Oklahoma City *Evening Gazette*: "Send deputies to Ned Christie's at once. We have him surrounded, but have not enough men. John Fields and Joe Bowers of our party are shot. Fields will die."[11]

To which Marshal Yoes replied: "Have wired everywhere for deputies. You will have lots of help tonight. Hold the fort by all means and get them this time."[12]

Creekmore summoned a number of men in Tahlequah for assistance, including the city marshal and High Sheriff Ben Knight. Knight was a full-blood who did not condone Christie's increasingly violent activities.

The *Evening Gazette* stated that Christie was supposed to have with him "Bear Paw and Walk-About, who are both desperate murderers and fugitives from justice."[13] This was not true, however. Thompson Bear Paw, twenty-nine, a Cherokee full-blood, was sitting at that moment in the Tahlequah National Prison, sentenced to be hanged for murder on December 30.[14] Walk-About, otherwise known as Little Arch, was certainly not a murderer, though he had been involved in illegal whiskey activities.[15]

The deputy marshals continued their assault upon the cabin throughout the night. Finally, they were "obliged to abandon the attempt."[16] Rusk reported to Marshal Yoes that all their efforts had little affect upon Ned's Fort.*

Marshal Yoes refused to give up. He now authorized a posse, under the management of Gus York, who was not an officer but, according to Yoes, was "well posted in the locality" where Christie lived.[17] York designated

----

*Following this run-in with Ned Christie, Creekmore became disillusioned with the marshal's service. So he joined with Henry Starr in two of his early petty store robberies at Lenapah and Sequoyah, in November 1892. But, according to Starr, Creekmore was overly fond of drink so Starr soon left him behind. "Of Creekmore," Starr commented in his autobiography, *Thrilling Events*, which he wrote while in the Colorado penitentiary, "I will say that he was brave and generous and possessed no little amount of intelligence. But he was foolish in combining two callings which were in direct conflict. He said he could not make any money riding marshal and besides he wanted to be a bandit, something on the order of Jesse James, but I had suspected that he meant to turn me in, and moved on without him."[18]

In March 1893, Creekmore surrendered to federal officers and was indicted on the two store robberies. Officers released him briefly on October 28 to marry Miss Cora Runyan at the home of his mother in Fort Smith and to have dinner. After that he went back to jail, and during Starr's trial, Creekmore turned state's evidence, and was set free.[19]

Deputy Marshal Gideon S. "Cap" White as head of the posse. From East Tennessee, Cap White had fought with the Union Cavalry as a captain during the Civil War. He stood and walked with a military bearing. His stylish clothes and enormous grey mustache added to his smart appearance.[20]

York and White laid their plans carefully. They knew their bullets wouldn't bother Christie, so they borrowed a cannon from an Army post in Kansas to take with them. They chose three-pound bullet-shaped projectiles which they believed would be more apt to penetrate the log walls of Christie's home. The cannon and ammunition were shipped on the train to Fayetteville, where they would be picked up and transported in a wagon with the deputies.[21] The cannon measured four feet in length with a one-inch bore. It was solidly mounted on an oak carriage and could be elevated with a screw wheel, or adjusted back and forth with a crowbar.[22] The deputies also obtained a quantity of dynamite.

Meanwhile, White set to work gathering his posse at Fayetteville, the stronghold of Maples sympathy. In a public meeting he climbed up on a chair and asked for volunteers.

Jesse Benton Easter, who lived on a nearby farm, refused to join the posse. "I have lost no Ned Christie," he asserted, "and from what I know of him, I think he is being persecuted."[23]

Others such as George Jefferson, Mack Peel, and Sam Maples were not so reluctant. It was well known in the community that the younger Maples had vowed years earlier if he ever got the chance to go after his father's murderer, he would. He believed wholeheartedly that Ned Christie was the guilty party and was eager to join the man hunt.

The remainder of the posse included: Deputy Marshals Paden and John Tolbert, former Georgians who now lived at Clarksville; Frank "Becky" Polk, a tall, raw-boned black man, also from Clarksville, who was a good shot and hired as a cook;[24] Enos Mills, blacksmith and federal lawman from Sulphur city;[25] Jim Birkett, a six-foot-three, dark-complexioned man, former sheriff of Washington County;[26] William Ellis, captain of the Coal and Iron Police, Hartshorne, Indian Territory, mining center;[27] Vint Gray, pioneer settler at Chouteau, Indian Territory, who had just established Vinita's first bank;[28] and last but not least, Deputy Marshal Wess Bowman.

Bowman, a native of Breathkitt County, Kentucky, had grown up in the Clarksville area. In 1952, when he was eighty-three-years-old, he granted an interview to a *Tulsa World* reporter. He said he could remember "like it was yesterday the day we got Ned Christie."

Bowman related that when young, he had long dreamed of becoming a law enforcement officer. Judge Issac Parker, "champion of justice and arch-enemy of crime," had sworn him in as a U.S. deputy marshal on February 10, 1891, when Bowman was twenty-two. The judge told him: "This is a dangerous job and you are a brave man or you would not be standing here before me. But you'll need more than courage to handle the job you've sworn to do. You'll need a good pistol, a good Winchester rifle and a good horse."[29]

Bowman said he knew what the judge meant, and he vowed to himself that he'd work hard at the job that he had chosen to follow.

That fall, he found himself assigned to the posse to get Christie. The group left Fayetteville on Tuesday, November 2, and headed for nearby West Fork. There they met Gus York. The next morning, the force of eleven men under White and York, set out for Ned's Fort with plenty of ammunition, arms, and provisions.[30]

Along the way more men joined the posse, until what was described as a "veritable army" was marching along. Among them rode E.B. Ratterree, Poteau, a huge man of great strength; Henry Clayland, seventeen, from Fort Smith; Frank Sarber, eighteen, whose father had been a deputy marshal in the early 1870s; Abe Allen; brothers Tol and Oscar Blackard; Deputy Marshal Tom Johnson; and Deputy Marshal William Smith, last Principal Chief of the Delaware, who was noted as a dangerous man with a gun and well versed in law.[31]

When the posse arrived that evening at J.F. Summer's store on the border of Indian Territory, it found Deputy Marshals Charley Copeland and Dave Rusk waiting, along with High Sheriff Ben Knight.

Cap White and Gus York had no intention of resting. They planned to arrive at Christie's fort before daylight. From the border of the Going Snake District, it would be Knight's job to guide them over the rough trail in the dark.

The posse set off again shortly after sunset. Early on the morning of November 3, they reached a point below Bitting Spring. Here they left the cannon and wagon of provisions to be brought up later.

The posse arrived at Ned's fort about 4:00 a.m.[32] Under the cover of darkness the men surrounded the outlaw's home and concealed themselves in the underbrush.[33]

As they waited in the cold, grey light of dawn, they had time to contemplate what was about to happen. Without a doubt, all knew they were on a particularly dangerous mission. Christie had only to catch a glimpse of them to put a bullet through them. But all were certain they would get him this time, for they did not intend to abandon their efforts until they had done so.

CHAPTER 16

The Final Assault

During the three weeks following the deputies' raid on October 12, Ned Christie had stayed close to the thick, sheltering walls of his fortified home. Likely, he knew it would be only a matter of time until the "government soldiers" came again. Each time their force had grown larger, and they seemed determined to have him one way or another. What happened during the course of this final assault on Christie was recorded in a variety of newspaper reports, interviews with friends and relatives, and court records. These can be pieced together to form a fairly accurate account of the event.

In the house with Christie on this ill-fated morning of November 3, 1892, were his wife Nancy, daughter Mary, and granddaughter Charlotte. There too were Little Arch and Charles Hare, "a young fullblood who had recently joined the gang,"[1] and a seven-year-old boy named Charles Grease,[2] who may have called Nancy "Aunt," per neighborhood custom, says Roy Hamilton. He adds family stories say Ned's son, James, was there also, but newspaper stories do not support this.

Outside, the moon set and all was quiet in the hour before dawn. The posse, stiff with cold, waited for the first light of morning. When it came, it showed promise of bringing a typical Indian Summer day, with a misty haze hanging over the land. The deputies must have wondered why the dogs, that usually surrounded the house, were quiet. Earlier the men had heard dogs barking down the hollow. Quietly, York gave his final orders. The deputies were to have two tasks: one, to keep Christie from escaping; two, to keep any of his friends

friends and relatives from slipping through the line to assist him.

The main point of command was centered on a rise above the ford on Bitting Creek, on the west side just south of the spring. Nearby, Cap White had positioned himself along with Heck Bruner, Wess Bowman, and Sam Maples. The other deputies had encircled the clearing, being careful to stay hidden behind the trees in the growing light.

Shortly after daylight, as the posse watched, "two women came out of the house and went back in."[3] Just at sunrise, "the door opened cautiously and Arch Wolf stepped out."[4] He started for the spring a few rods distant. Before reaching it he was ordered to surrender. But "the only reply he gave was a shower of bullets, none of which, however, took effect. The fire was returned, and several bullets crushed through him."[5]

Wounded in the leg and with a broken arm, Little Arch "fell but he got up and staggered back toward the cabin."[6] Another "shot glanced from his head. He succeeded in reaching the door which was quickly opened and closed as he entered."[7] After this initial action, "Christie whooped as he always did when a fight was on,"[8] and a hail of bullets blazed from the portholes. The deputies returned the fire.

Gus York called for Ned to surrender. As usual, he refused. Wanting to be sure the crafty outlaw understood the danger of his position, York asked Sheriff Ben Knight to repeat his warning in Cherokee. Again Christie responded with a fusillade of bullets. White told him if he was going to fight, to send out his women and children.

Like always when a fight was on, Christie had sent his family to the root cellar, out of the way of flying bullets. Now he ordered them to leave the house. Mary and Nancy hurried out with Charlotte, but "for some reason Charley Grease...didn't run out with the rest," according to Tuxie Miller.[9]

The Oklahoma City *Evening Gazette* also took note that the "females of the Christie family were allowed to retreat," and added that "during which a young son* of Christie was intercepted while he was trying to take to his father two boxes of cartridges.[10]

"The active work then began. The outlaws inside the house kept up a perfect fusillade of bullets all during the day."[11]

A crowd of friends and relatives gathered below the wagon ford. They watched in silence. The heavy smoke from the black powder used in the cartridges drifted in the November air, stinging their nostrils.

"The marshals kept demanding the surrender of the outlaw and his two confederates, and promised them good treatment, but met with refusal and defiance every time," the *Evening Gazette* reported.[12]

Christie "laughed at them for he was winning." Ned and Little Arch "thought it comical that the government soldiers would go to all that trouble just to capture a couple of poor Indians..."[13]

"Even the women who had come out of the house, made sport of the officers for their audacity for trying to capture Christie," the *Arkansas Gazette* stated.[14]

Watt Christie, Ned's father, stood among those waiting on the creek bank. White sent Ben Knight to Watt to entreat his son to give up. But Watt refused, for he "could see no evil in his son."[15]

———

*Though not named in newspaper accounts, most likely this was James Christie, Ned's only legitimate son, who is not mentioned in newspaper accounts as being in the house that morning. Wiley Wolf also stated that a group of young men had been camping at Bitting Spring that night while hunting, when someone arrived to tell them deputy marshals were in the area hunting Ned Christie.[16] If James Christie was with this group of young men and Christie's pack of dogs followed him, this would explain why the dogs did not bark on this morning, to warn Christie of the presence of the deputy marshals.

Mary approached the deputies. Perhaps thinking of Charles Grease as well as attempting to help her father, she told Ben Knight, "Baby in fort." He translated her words to the deputies, expressing his doubt. "Indian women would never leave baby in fort," he said. He snatched her apron, which she held clutched before her. In its folds, he found five boxes of .44 caliber cartridges. Mary ran off into the brush before they could stop her.[17]

The deputies "kept it up at long range until 1 o'clock, when the cannon arrived."[18] It was set on a big "post oak stump" across Bitting Creek in the field near Christie's first homesite.[19] The deputies fired thirty-eight rounds at the cabin, but the cannon "proved too weak to knock down the fort."[20] Wess Bowman later related:

> The cabin walls were too tough for the cannonballs. They just bounced off, barely missing the deputies who had the cabin surrounded. Finally the man in charge decided to use a heavier charge of powder. He packed it in and then fired the weapon. But the charge was too heavy, and the cannon was blown to pieces.[21]

The sounds of the battle attracted an even larger crowd as the day wore on. The *Evening Gazette* reported:

> ...several marshals are wounded. The mail carrier who passes through the Caney mountains near Christie's house, reports he met a wagon loaded with provisions and ammunition and the marshals would positively not withdraw until their man was captured dead or alive.[22]

The fight continued until dark. The deputies held a conference. They were getting nowhere. Their guns were useless against the stout walls of the cabin. They would have to try something else.

They determined to use dynamite. But how could they get close enough for it to be effective? Someone thought of Christie's wagon setting in the yard. Perhaps they could use it as a shield. The *Evening Gazette* stated: "When a cloud came up darkening the light of the moon, Will Smith and Charlie Copeland slipped up to the wagon within 22 feet of the house and built a fortification with fence rails."[23]

The deputies prepared a "bundle containing more than a dozen sticks of dynamite," and Charlie Copeland volunteered to set the dynamite.[24]

"A vigilant watch was kept by the marshals during the long hours of the night. Directly after the moon went down,"[25] "while part of the party kept up the fire on one side of the house, Charlie Copeland ran up on another side and placed the dynamite."[26] Attached to the explosive was "a long fuse which was not fired till daylight."[27]

The resulting explosion "wrecked the house and knocked out one corner,"[28] "leaving a hole big enough that you could ride a horse through...and the sound of the explosion was heard in Tahlequah."[29]

"The building began to burn," and those within "were again asked to surrender, but refused and kept up the fight."[30]

By now Christie must have known it was a fight to death. Little Arch was wounded and the flames were crackling around them. They retreated to the root cellar.* Then the burning roof fell in.[31] Arch Wolf's hair

---

*The whereabouts of Charles Grease at this time is unknown. Most likely he was in the root cellar and no one had time to look after him. Some believed he was shot and killed early in the fight.

Historian T.L. Ballenger, displays cannon ball which was shot at Ned Christie's fortified home during the final battle. The cannonball was given to Ballenger by Goback Christie, Ned's youngest brother. *Photo by Bonnie Speer.*

Posse men rest beside sawmill following the killing of Ned Christie. Left to right, Frank "Becky" Polk (cook), Policeman Birkett, Oscar Blackard, Frank Sarber, Vint Gray, Tol Blackard, J.M. (Mack) Peel, Harvey Clayland, George Jefferson, and Paden Tolbert. *Courtesy Phillip Steele and the Cecil Atchison Collection.*

119

Members of the posse who shot Ned Christie, pose with the body of Christie on the front steps of the Fort Smith courthouse. 1) Paden Tolbert, 2) Capt. G.S. White, 3) Coon Ratteree, 4) Enos Mills, 5) Ned Christie, 6) Thomas Johnson, 7) Charles Copeland, 8) Heck Bruner. Photo taken November 3, 1893. *Courtesy Western History Collections, University of Oklahoma Library.*

Posse members who shot Ned Christie pose for a formal portrait in Fort Smith. Standing, from left: Wess Bowman, Abe Allen, John Tolbert, Bill Smith, Tom Johnson. Sitting: Dave Rusk, Heck Bruner, Paden Tolbert, Charles Copeland, and Captain G.S. White. *Courtesy Western History Collections, University of Oklahoma Library.*

caught fire. Burning timbers struck Charles Hare. No longer could they remain where they were.

Thick smoke from the burning house enveloped the clearing. "While the blaze was at its fiercest, Christie was seen to emerge from under the floor and firing his six-shooter at the nearest deputies. He started to run, but was ordered to halt."[32] For a moment, he and Ben Knight gazed at each other without firing, then Christie "veered away."[33]

He went on "with a Winchester in his hands and a pistol in his belt, firing as he ran."[34]

In the smoke and confusion, he almost got away. He "got through the yard gate and started running down the road by the side of the fence like some scared fox."[35]

Wess Bowman related: "Just as the smoke was beginning to clear away, I heard a yell and saw Ned Christie running from the cabin. He came straight at me and the two other deputies, firing his rifle as he came."[36]

The deputies returned the fire, riddling Christie's body with bullets.* Legend says he fell on the rocks between two blackgum saplings,[39] but not before Bowman received a memento he was to carry the rest of his life. "The last shot Christie fired went off almost in my face," he said. "The bullet missed me, but my face was burned by the rifle blast and particles of powder were imbedded in my skin."[40]

In the sudden stillness which followed, as the deputies gathered around Christie, Sam Maples ran up, and in a frenzy of revenge, emptied his revolver into his vanquished foe.[41]

------

*Wess Bowman is generally credited with killing Ned Christie but Allene J. Davis states that according to her grandfather, Goback Christie, who was the youngest brother of Ned and present in the crowd which gathered on the opposite side of Bitting Creek that morning to watch the battle, a young boy, holding the horses in the ravine was the one who shot Christie as he ran through the brush.

This story was also told by Jefferson Tindall in a 1970 interview.[37] It is interesting to note in the picture taken of the deputies beside the sawmill, shortly after the killing of Ned Christie, that there is a very young looking boy sitting on the ground in the middle of the picture, who is identified in Phillip Steele's book, *The Last Cherokee Warriors*, as Frank Sarber. In *Iron Men*, C.J. McKennon credits Sarber with being eighteen years old, and Harry Clayland, seventeen, the youngest member of the posse. Wess Bowman was twenty-two years old at the time but looked much younger. He was identified by one writer as "the beardless youth."[38] So he may have been mistaken by those in the crowd that morning, for the "young boy" holding the horses.

CHAPTER 17

Aftermath

The Indian women waiting on the knoll above the ford trilled in mourning. The sun rose, and a light wind scattered the drifting smoke. The shattered tops of the post oak trees surrounding the clearing testified to the fury of the battle which had raged here but a few minutes before.

With Ned Christie taken care of, "the officers turned their attention to the burning building and discovered Charlie Hare trying to escape."[1] The youth had been badly burned, and he was "arrested for resisting the U.S. marshals."[2]

First reports were that "the body of Wolf, who had been wounded early in the morning, was burned to a crisp in the building." The crowd of spectators and deputies milled around the dead Christie and marveled at the morning's happening. The *Arkansas Gazette* said the "three men had kept up the battle with the deputies for 24 hours, and fought to the death. None of the marshal's men were killed."[3]

In a festive mood, the deputies strapped Christie's body to a door from his cabin and carried him to their camp. The terms for collecting the reward stated that Christie had to be delivered to the Fort Smith jail before they could collect any money. A photographer, who was in the crowd, took pictures of the deputies resting beside a sawmill. Likely it was the same one Christie used in building his log fort. After "a hearty meal fixed by Becky Polk," the deputies loaded the remains of "the noted desperado and adopted son, Charley Hare," into their wagon, and hauled them to Fayetteville.[4]

There they "threw him [Christie] out on the sidewalk," and a crowd gathered to stare. Jesse Benton Easter, who had refused to join the posse a few days before, "was just exasperated."[5]

New rumors circulated. The Oklahoma City *Evening Gazette* reported: "There is some doubt about the rewards for Christie being paid as they were being offered for him alive, though it is presumed the friends of Maples would probably reward the brave men for the risks they had taken."[6]

Deputy Marshal Cap White found the local doctor and asked him to issue a certificate of death.* The certificate stated simply:

> This is to certify that I have examined the corpse of Ned Christie and I am satisfied that he came to his death from gun shot wounds and not from any contagious or infectious disease.
> Fayetteville, Ark., Nov. 5th 1892.
> [signed] H.D. Wood, M.D.[7]

On Sunday morning, Charles Hare, along with the body of Ned Christie, was taken on to Fort Smith "from Fayetteville where they had missed the train on Saturday."[8]

The *Fort Smith Call* remarked:

> Monday the corpse was placed in the front entrance of the jail and the public were [sic]

---

*The original document is in the possession of Allene J. Davis.

allowed to see the disfigured tenement [sic] of clay so recently occupied by a more contorted soul.

Christie was a fullblood Indian and his countenance and general makeup is about an ideal one would have of the original blood thirsty savage of the "western wilds."[9]

A photographer set up his camera to take souvenir photos of Christie's body. Deputy Marshal Hugh Harp "laid his rifle in Christie's hands because he thought any picture of the desperate outlaw should depict him holding a weapon."[10]

Judge Issac Parker personally congratulated each of the posse men who had accompanied Christie's body to Fort Smith, for his part in killing the notorious outlaw. After this, the deputies went down to Gannaway's Studio for a formal portrait to commemorate the event.

Christie's body remained on public display until that evening, when it was placed on the 4:00 p.m. train and shipped to Fort Gibson.[11] There it was claimed by the outlaw's father. Watt Christie buried his son in the Christie family cemetery near his home. Ned's brothers built a small wooden house over Ned's grave to protect and comfort his spirit, as was the custom of the Cherokees. But unlike the others in the cemetery, Ned's grave house was painted black.[12]

The *Arkansas Gazette* eulogized the ill-fated "outlaw" in these words: "Christie was as notorious in some respects as the Dalton boys, but to his credit be it said he never made a practice of robbing people. He was a quiet, peaceable man, but his career of crime commenced when he killed Maples."[13]

Marshal Jacob Yoes wrote a full report of the killing of Ned Christie to the Attorney-General, Washington, D.C., and asked that the $1,000 reward be paid to the posse (see Appendix).

Subsequently during the last week of December, Gus York received the money as requested. After paying all expenses, he divided the balance equally among the posse members. Each man received $74.[14]

Dick Humphrey, listed in court records as a witness in the murder of Deputy Marshal Daniel Maples, never testified in court because the case never came to trial. In 1918, he told his story to a reporter from the *Daily Oklahoman* and cleared Ned Christie's name. For years, fear of Bub Trainor had sealed the blacksmith's lips, as well as a few others who knew the facts.[15]

Then Trainor died. The *Vinita Leader* reported his death on January 9, 1896: "Bub Trainor, well known here, was killed at Talala on Christmas night, by 4 negroes. It was a plot, and 4 shotguns did the work."[16]

But even after this event, Humphrey was still afraid to tell what he knew, without court protection, for fear of Trainor's gang. With the passing years, the matter likely seemed less urgent. Humphrey never forgot about it though, and wanted to set the record straight before he died. He was eighty-seven-years-old when his opportunity finally came.

In Rabbit Trap, Tuxie Milller said it was soon determined that it was not Arch Wolf who had been "burned to death under that floor in the cabin,"[17] but Charley Grease, the seven-year-old boy who called Nancy aunt. Little Arch had lost all of his hair in the fire but had escaped and fled northward with the help of friends. He and Charles Hare were both indicted in the Fort Smith court for "assault with intent to kill."[18]

Charles Hare was brought to trial in March 1893. Found guilty as charged, he served three years at hard labor in the Illinois State Reformatory.[19]

Arch Wolf was arrested in November that year in a Chicago hotel lobby by U.S. deputy marshals.[20] Returned to Fort Smith by Charley Copeland, he, too, was found guilty as charged. He was sentenced to the

Kings County Penitentiary, Brooklyn, for two years at hard labor, plus three years for illegal whiskey selling on two counts.[21]

Locked up behind bars far from home, in a place where the Cherokee language was not spoken, Arch Wolf developed "extreme melancholy." On August 29, 1895, he was admitted to the Government Hospital for the Insane in Washington.[22]

It was expected he would be there for three months but the time lengthened into years. His father, Jack Wolf, and grandfather, Arch Christie, with the help of Charles E. Young, a schoolteacher at Stony Point, wrote a number of letters to the superintendent of the asylum pleading for information. Said one:

> You please let me know What they gone Do for Him my Grand Son Arch Wolf, they the [sic] gone Hold Him till time out or they Turn him out. Want you let let [sic] me know that. I am yours Friend
> [signed] Arch Christie[23]

In 1896, Arch Wolf's family applied to the President of the United States for a pardon, however, their request was denied. Two years later, they heard that Little Arch had died, but this information soon proved false. It was not until 1903 that he was released and returned home.[24]

Shortly after the death of Ned Christie, Sam Maples went to California then on to Canada with a friend on a wagon train, where he died in a "black blizzard."[25]

What happened to James Christie? The *Watonga Republican* reported his violent death on July 12, 1893:

JAMES CHRISTIE MURDERED
TAHLEQUAH, Ind. Ter., July 6 — Last evening while on the road near his home about

twelve miles east of this place, James Christie was attacked by unknown assassins and killed. His head was severed from his body. The murdered man was a son of the notorious Ned Christie, who gave the United States officers so much trouble until killed in his fort last fall. He is also a nephew of Bill Christie, who is in jail at this place, sentenced to hang on the 18th of August.[26]

According to Roy Hamilton, a second newspaper stated James was to testify in court against a fellow Cherokee, who met him along the road and effectively silenced him, when James refused to drop his testimony So, raised in an atmosphere of violence, James died in the same manner, fifteen years old at the time.

Thus the saga of Ned Christie ended. Soon after his death, the legend of his exploits began to grow. Today, it still lives in the flinty hills of eastern Oklahoma that he called home. While we may never know the entire truth about Ned Christie's criminal record, his bravery cannot be questioned, for he fought to the death rather than be arrested for a crime which it seems that he did not commit. Some even say that, like a true martyr, he willingly sacrificed his life in the end so those in the burning house might have a chance to escape. It is also to Christie's credit that he was not a born killer, for many times with his deadly aim he could have killed the deputies who were stalking him, which bears out the belief of those who claimed he was shooting only in self-defense.

Memory of Ned Christie remained long in the hearts of his neighbors. Jefferson Tindall related:

The white man tried to make a ukaga out of Ned, as they have all Indians for 400 years and still it does not work. The memory of a good man forced into a way of life he did not want is wonderfully preserved in the hearts of his people. The memory of thousands of whites who were great in their time have long since been forgotten.[27]

Edward Hines summed up Christie's life this way:

He was a very clever man. If he had been a soldier he would have been one of the greatest of generals. Ned Christie was one of the bravest in the South West.[28]

In time the land allotted to Watt Christie, which contained the Christie family cemetery, passed into the hands of white men. One took advantage of the fenced cemetery to use it as a calf and hog pen. The animals knocked over the headstones and broke them. In 1979, a new owner removed the fence and piled the headstones to one side. Then he plowed up the land and planted potatoes over the graves. Learning of this desecration, Allene J. Davis, a grandniece of Christie's, went to the owner and obtained permission to re-fence the cemetery and re-establish the headstones. When she arrived at the cemetery with other family members, she found that Christie's marker had been broken and part of it stolen. The missing piece was eventually located and recovered. The cemetery was fenced again and the headstones set back in place, though the family had to guess at the exact location of the various graves.

All except that of Ned Christie.

Indomitable in death as he had been in life, his headstone clung tenaciously to its original site, entwined in the roots of the tall oak tree which had sheltered it for many years.

"Little Arch" Wolf, a member of Ned Christie's gang, was the son of Ned's sister, Betsy Wolf. *Courtesy Phillip Steele and the Cecil Atchison Collection.*

Desecrated Christie family cemetery and broken tombstone of Ned Christie. *Photo by Bonnie Speer.*

AUTHOR'S NOTE

Was Ned Christie wrongfully accused of the multitude of crimes some said he committed? No charges against him, except for the alleged murder of Deputy Dan Maples, can be found in the archives of the Fort Smith federal court, now preserved in the Federal Archives and Records Center, Fort Worth, Texas. Marshal Yoes informally accused Christie, in his final report, of introducing whiskey, a federal charge, and of robbing stores and killing and wounding a number of Cherokee people, which would have been a Cherokee Nation charge. If the latter was true, a preliminary search of Cherokee records at the Oklahoma State Historical Society should have revealed these charges, yet none have surfaced except for the Palone case. In addition there are contradictory statements between Yoes' report, which claims Christie was guilty of robbery, and that of the *Arkansas Gazette*, which says he wasn't.

Which one do we believe? What of his friends and relatives who continued to uphold Ned Christie's honor for years following his death? Admittedly, oral interviews taken fifty to eighty years after the event should be considered with caution, for names and facts are often confused. For instance W.G.D. Hines in the Indian-Pioneer interviews taken in 1937 and 1938 was quoted as saying that it was commonly remarked at the time of Christie's troubles that Heck Bruner was the deputy marshal Christie wanted to shoot instead of Heck Thomas or Bub Trainor. Nat Dickerson claimed that Heck Bruner was the one who shot Christie. Even Christie's brother-in-law, James R. Padgett, erroneously

131

stated that at the time of Maples' death, Christie was a "messenger boy" for the Cherokee legislature (though he may have been earlier).

Even today, caution must be exercised in regard to oral history. When I first talked to Allene J. Davis, she was insistent that her grandfather, Goback Christie, believed Ned guilty of Maples' death, yet T.L. Ballenger's statement plainly refuted this statement. He said that Goback was one of Ned's staunchest supporters, who referred to him as a "good man." Bettie Maples Halsell, when I talked to her, refused to believe that Christie was not the one who killed her great-grandfather, Dan Maples. Yet she had in her possession a clipping written by Fred E. Sutton (1922) suggesting that such may have been the case. In *The Last Cherokee Warriors*, Phillip Steele quotes Bill Christie, Jr., a grandson of Watt Christie's, as saying that between the years of 1892 and 1895 he was often in and around Ned's home when marshals attacked. This is in error as Ned died in 1892.

Nevertheless, many of those who granted interviews to the WPA workers in the 1930s had personal knowledge of Ned Christie. Others interviewed during the Doris Duke project in the late 1960s were direct descendants of those who were contemporaries of Christie. Some validity must be accorded their statements, especially those which can be supported by archival documents and contemporary newspaper accounts. In particular, I found the interviews with C.B. Rhodes (1937) and Stanley A. Clark (1937) to be the most reliable. Rhodes, who was a lawman, did not participate in the capture of Ned Christie, but served with most of the men who did. Two interviews with Tuxie Miller (1937), a neighbor of Christie's, also seem to be well founded, as well as those of Eli Wilson (1937) and William Hugh Winder (1937).

Most of the erroneous stories about Ned Christie (that he and John Parris had been returning from Dog Town when Deputy Maples ordered them to halt and Ned Christie shot him) can be attributed to John Parris himself. This is the tale he concocted to save his own skin when it looked as if the murder might be pinned on him. Numerous writers since that time have simply picked up this story and printed it for truth, without bothering to check the facts.

APPENDIX

DEPARTMENT OF JUSTICE
United States Marshal's Office
WESTERN DISTRICT OF ARKANSAS
Fort Smith, Ark., Nov. 12th, 1892

Hon. W. H. H. Miller,
Attorney-General U.S.,
Washington, D.C.

Dear Sir:-

The man Ned Christie, who defied the U.S. and Indian authorities for five years successfully has at last been brought to a halt, though I am sorry to say that he had to be killed in the attempt to capture him.

Marshal Carroll who had a deputy killed by him made several efforts for his capture but failed. I made a number of attempts. My deputies have been after him from the time I first took charge of the office up to the time that he was killed. In October, 1889, an organized deputy force with posse succeeded in locating him in one of his strongholds, and attacked him early in the morning. Upon the call to surrender he immediately fired from between the logs of the house, severely wounding Deputy L.P. Isbell, crippling him for life. The deputies succeeded in setting fire to the house, but Christie remained until shot in the head, and would have burned up had it not been for the timely arrival of some of his women after the deputy force had left thinking he had escaped. As soon as he recovered from his wound he again commenced his career of crime

134

introducing whiskey by the wagon load and robbing stores with impunity. He had killed and wounded a number of Cherokee People, and they attempted his capture on various occasions, but signally failed. If the force organized for his capture was large he managed in some way to be informed of it, and get out of the way, if the force was small he would make a fight from one of his log houses, generally resulting in a victory for him. Last fall he was located at a certain place, and I organized a force myself and went with them in person. It was done secretly, and in a very short time, but when we arrived at the place the bird had flown. We demolished a stone fort near the house where he was located. Since then every effort has resulted in wounding some of the men in my force. Very recently two of the posse attacking the same place were wounded. William Fields was shot through the neck, and Joe Powrs [sic] in the foot. Upon the return of that unsuccessful raid the party who have just returned with his body was organized, under the management of Gus York, who was not an officer, but was well posted in the locality where Christie lived. I enclose you a newspaper account of their trip, and what occurred. It is nearly a complete statement, except that it does not contain all the names of the parties engaged, and leaves out some important facts that I will mention. First, on the morning and during the first day after arrival at the place they called to Christie to surrender a number of times, both in English and in Cherokee, but wach [sic] time he would answer with a yell, and by shooting. Also, when he finally came out of the burning house he yelled "damned white marshals" and firing his six-shooter at the nearest deputies.

Now, in behalf of Mr. Gus York I would ask that the reward offered by you be paid to him. He will reimburse the deputies who are out so much time and money. The amount of money expended at various times by different officers and citizens for the captrue [sic] of this man is at least three times the amount of the reward. The hardships and dangers endured in this behalf can hardly be paid with money, but the thousand dollars offered by you will at least partially reimburse the people who have borne the expense, suffered the hardships and endangered their lives in the interest of the Government. I therefore earnestly request that the reward offered in your letter of October 15, 1890, initial "A.G. 3425. 1887," be paid to Mr. Gus York, who was in charge of the last party, and who will do what is right to the people who are entitled to their respective proportion of it.

I also enclose an identification of the body of Ned Christie, and an order from Judge Parker. The body of Ned Christie was delivered to me at the U.S. Jail at Fort Smith, Arkansas.

Begging your early and favorable consideration, I am,

Yours respectfully,

(Dictated.)

Jacob Yoes
U.S. Marshal
West Dist Ark.[1]

ENDNOTES

Introduction

[1]Outlaw, Ned Christie, "Cherokee Outlaw of Indian Territory," ADS 2-24-38, Service Bureau of the South, Research Department, FTP, Oklahoma, University of Wyoming, Laramie.

[2]Conley, Robert D., *Back To Malachi*, Doubleday & Company, New York, New York, 1986, Author's Note.

Prologue

[1]Foreman, Carolyn, *Park Hill*, The Press of the Star Printery, Inc., Muskogee, Oklahoma, 1948, p. 173.

[2] *Ibid.*

[3]Interview of Alex Matheson, Vol. 61, p. 24, Western History Collections, University of Oklahoma Library.

[4]*The Cherokee Advocate*, April 27, 1887.

Chapter 1

[1]Letter, Jacob Yoes to W.H.H. Miller, Attorney General, Washington, D. C., November 12, 1892, National Archives and Records Service, Washington, D.C.

[2]Steele, Phillip, *The Last Cherokee Warriors*, Pelican Publishing Company, Gretna, Louisiana, 1974, p. 69.

[3]*Fort Smith Call* as reprinted in *The Muskogee Phoenix*, November 10, 1892.

[4]Tombstone, Ned Christie. Also see Steele, Phillip, *The Last Cherokee Warriors*, Pelican Publishing Company, Gretna, Louisiana, 1974, p. 72.

[5]Interview of Elmira Stevens by Wylie Thornton, February 4, 1938, #12893, Vol. 87, p. 278, typescript, Doris Duke Indian Oral History Collection, Western History Collections, University of Oklahoma Library.

[6]Steele, Phillip, *The Last Cherokee Warriors*, Pelican Publishing Company, Gretna, Louisiana, 1974, p. 72.

[7]Cherokee Valuations, North Carolina, 1836, Welch & Garrett, No. 14, National Archives and Records Service, Washington, D.C.

[8]Interview of Amos Christie by J. W. Tyner, June 12, 1969, Vol. 12, T-476-1, typescript, in The Doris Duke Indian Oral History Collection in the Western History Collections, University of Oklahoma Library.

[9]*Ibid.*

[10]First Cherokee Mounted Rifles, roster, Oklahoma Historical Society.

[11]*Ibid.*

[12]Original enlistment papers of Watt Christie in possession of Allene J. Davis, his great-granddaughter.

[13]Steele, Phillip, *The Last Cherokee Warriors*, Pelican Publishing Company, Gretna, Louisiana, 1974, p. 73.

[14]Woodward, Grace Steele, *The Cherokees*, University of Oklahoma Press, Norman, 1963, p. 316.

[15]*Daily Oklahoman* (Oklahoma City), June 9, 1918.

[16]Cherokee Census Records, 1900, Roll No. 29987, Oklahoma Historical Society.

[17]*Ibid.*, Roll No. 1488.

[18]Cherokee Census Records, 1880, Oklahoma Historical Society

[19]Cherokee Census Rolls, 1900, Roll No. 1488, Oklahoma Historical Society.

[20]Harman, Samuel W., *Hell On the Border, He Hanged Eighty-Eight Men*, edited by Jack Gregory and Rennard Strickland, Indian Heritage Publishers, Muskogee, 1971, p. 94.

[21]*The Cherokee Advocate*, November 14, 1885.

[22]*Fort Smith Elevator*, April 22, 1887.

[23]*Ibid.*

[24]Proceedings of the Executive Council, Vol. 710, p. 56, Cherokee Nation Papers, Indian History Collection, Oklahoma Historical Society.

[25]*Ibid.*

Chapter 2

[1]Letter, Mrs. Bettie Halsell, Fayetteville, Ark., to Bonnie Speer, March 17, 1980.

[2]*Fort Smith Elevator*, May 13, 1887.

[3]Shirley, Glenn, *Law West of Fort Smith*, Henry Holt and Company, New York, New York, 1957, p. 23.

[4]*Fort Smith Elevator*, April 15, 1887.

[5]Wardell, Morris L., *A Political History of the Cherokee Nation*, University of Oklahoma Press, Norman, Oklahoma, 1938, p. 309.

[6]*Ibid.*, p. 221.

[7]Shirley, Glenn, *Law West of Fort Smith*, Henry Holt and Company, New York, New York, 1957, p. 23.

[8]Interview of Fred Palone, Vol. 6, p. 136, Indian-Pioneer Papers, Western History Collections, University of Oklahoma Library.

[9]*Fort Smith Elevator*, July 29, 1887.

[10]Interview of Ben Hartness by Boyce Timmons, Field Worker, Vol. 15, T-460, typescript, in the Doris Duke Indian Oral History Collection, Western History Collections, University of Oklahoma.

[11]*The Cherokee Advocate*, July 6, 1887.

[12]Matheson, Mrs. Anna C. Trainor, *Chronicles of Oklahoma*, Vol. 8, p. 101.

[13]*Ibid.*

[14]Interview of Ben Hartness by Boyce Timmons, Field Worker, Vol. 15, T-460, typescript in The Doris Duke Collection, Indian Oral History Collection, Western History Collections, University of Oklahoma Library.

[15]*Ibid.*

[16]*Ibid.*

[17]*Ibid.*

[18]*Ibid.*

[19]*Indian Chieftain* (Vinita, Cherokee Nation), March 17, 1887.

[20]*Ibid.*

[21]*Fort Smith Elevator*, April 15, 1887.

[22]*Ibid.*, May 13, 1887.

23*Siloam Springs Herald* (Arkansas), May 13, 1887.

24Phone conversation, Mrs. Beatrice Maples Jones with Bonnie Speer, February 11, 1980. Also see Phillip Steele, *The Last Cherokee Warriors*, Pelican Publishing Company, Gretna, Louisiana, 1974, p. 80.

25*Indian Chieftain* (Vinita, Cherokee Nation), May 12, 1887.

26*Daily Oklahoman* (Oklahoma City), June 9, 1918.

27*Fayetteville Democrat* (Arkansas), May 13, 1887.

Chapter 3

1Proceedings of the Executive Council, Vol. 710, p. 56, Cherokee Nation Papers, Indian History Collection, Oklahoma State Historical Society.

2*Cherokee Advocate* (Tahlequah, Cherokee Nation), April 14, 1900.

3Records of the Cherokee Nation, Court Criminal Cases, p. 95, Indian History Collection, Oklahoma Historical Society.

4Interview of T.L. Ballenger by Bonnie Speer, December 6, 1979.

5Records of the Cherokee Nation, Court Criminal Cases, p. 95, Oklahoma Historical Society.

6*Cherokee Advocate* (Tahlequah, Cherokee Nation), November 3, 1886.

7Interview of Stanley A. Clark, by Jas. S. Buchanan, October 30, 1937, Indian-Pioneer Papers, Vol. 18, p. 204, in the Western History Collections, University of Oklahoma Library.

8Cherokee Census Roll, 1892, Indian History Collection, Oklahoma Historical Society.

9Criminal Records Fort Smith, various jackets, Record Group 21, United States District Court for the Western District of Arkansas, Federal Archives and Records Center, Fort Worth, Texas.

10*Daily Oklahoman*, June 9, 1918.

11*Ibid.*

12*Fort Smith Elevator*, May 20, 1887.

13*Ibid.*

14*Daily Oklahoman* (Oklahoma City), June 9, 1918.

Chapter 4

[1]Interview of Billy Parris, Vol. 69, p. 365, Indian-Pioneer Papers, Western History Collections, University of Oklahoma Library.

[2]Criminal Records Fort Smith, various jackets, Record Group 21, United States District Court for the Western District of Arkansas, National Archives, Regional Repository, Fort Worth, Texas.

[3]*Daily Oklahoman* (Oklahoma City), June 9, 1918.

[4]*Ibid.*

[5]Census Records, Cherokee Rolls, 1890, Freedmen, Indian History Collection, Oklahoma Historical Society.

[6]*Ibid.*

[7]*Ibid.*

[8]*Daily Oklahoman* (Oklahoma City), June 9, 1918.

[9]*Indian Chieftain* (Vinita, Cherokee Nation), May 12, 1887.

[10]*Fort Smith Elevator*, May 13, 1887.

[11]*Indian Chieftain* (Vinita, Cherokee Nation), May 12, 1887.

[12]*Fort Smith Elevator*, May 20, 1887.

[13]*Daily Oklahoman* (Oklahoma City), June 9, 1918.

[14]*Indian Chieftain* (Vinita, Cherokee Nation), May 12, 1887.

[15]*Daily Oklahoman* (Oklahoma City), June 9, 1918.

[16]*Indian Chieftain* (Vinita, Cherokee Nation), May 12, 1887.

[17]*Ibid.*

[18]*Fort Smith Elevator*, May 13, 1887.

[19]*Indian Chieftain* (Vinita, Cherokee Nation), May 12, 1887.

Chapter 5

[1]*Daily Oklahoman* (Oklahoma City), June 9, 1918.

[2]Interview of T.L. Ballenger by Bonnie Speer, December 6, 1979. Also see T. L. Ballenger, *Around Tahlequah Council Fires*, Motter Bookbinding Co., Muskogee, Oklahoma, 1935, p. 135, and the *Daily Oklahoman*, June 9, 1918.

[3]*Fort Smith Elevator*, May 13, 1887.

[4]*Indian Chieftain* (Vinita, Cherokee Nation), May 18, 1887.

[5]*Fort Smith Elevator*, May 13, 1887.

[6]*Ibid.*

[7]*Fort Smith Elevator*, May 18, 1887.

[8]Shirley, Glenn, *Law West of Fort Smith*, Henry Holt and Company, New York, New York, 1957, p. 79.

[9]*Fort Smith Elevator*, July 1, 1887.

[10]*Daily Oklahoman* (Oklahoma City), June 9, 1918.

[11]Criminal Record Jackets, 1866-1896, John Parris, RG 21, Western District of Arkansas, Fort Smith, Federal Archives and Records Center, Fort Worth, Texas.

[12]Interview of Tuxie Miller by Annie R. Faulton, August 16, 1938, "Ned Christie, Cherokee Fugitive," Service Bureau of the Southwest Research Department, FTP, Oklahoma, University of Wyoming, Laramie.

[13]*Fayetteville Democrat* (Arkansas), May 13, 1887.

[14]Wright, Mildred, "Life of Ned Christie," typescript, Cherokee Room, Northeastern University, Tahlequah, Oklahoma.

[15]*Fort Smith Elevator*, May 16, 1887.

[16]Cherokee Records, National Council, Extra Session, May 4, 1887, p. 208, Oklahoma Historical Society.

[17]Interview of Eli Wilson by Wylie Thornton, July 26, 1937, Vol. 99, p. 142, Indian-Pioneer Papers, Western History Collections, University of Oklahoma Library.

[18]*Daily Oklahoman* (Oklahoma City), June 9, 1918.

Chapter 6

[1]*Fort Smith Elevator*, May 20, 1887.

[2]Personal Papers, Thomas family, owned by Beth Thomas Meeks, Norman, Oklahoma; also see *Heck Thomas, My Papa*, Beth Thomas Meeks with Bonnie Speer, Levite of Apache, 1988, pp. 10-12.

[3]*Fort Smith Elevator*, January 25, 1887.

[4]*Ibid.*, May 27, 1887.

[5]*Muskogee Indian Journal*, May 26, 1887.

[6]*Fort Smith Elevator*, May 27, 1887.

[7]*Ibid.*

[8]Wardell, Morris L., *A Political History of the Cherokee Nation*, University of Oklahoma Press, Norman, 1938, p. 309.

[9]*Ibid.*

[10]Interview of Robin Vann by L.W. Wilson, November 12, 1937, Indian-Pioneer Papers, Vol. 86, p. 472, Western History Collections, University of Oklahoma.

[11]*Ibid.*

[12]*Tahlequah Telephone*, June 10, 1887.

[13]Criminal Records, 1866-1896, Jacket #187, Record Group 21, Western District of Arkansas, Fort Smith, Federal Archives and Records Center, Fort Worth, Texas.

[14]*Ibid.*

[15]*Siloam Springs Herald* (Arkansas) as reprinted in the *Tahlequah Telephone*, June 10, 1887.

[16]*Tahlequah Telephone*, June 10, 1887.

[17]Cherokee Records, Records of the National Council, Extra Session, May 1887, p. 208, Indian History Collection, Oklahoma Historical Society.

[18]*Cherokee Advocate*, July 6, 1887.

[19]*Fort Smith Elevator*, July 8, 1887.

[20]*Cherokee Advocate*, July 6, 1887.

[21]*Ibid.*

[22]*Fort Smith Elevator*, July 8, 1887.

[23]*Ibid.*

[24]*Ibid.*, July 1, 1887.

[25]Ibid.

[26]*Ibid.*, July 8, 1887.

[27]Common Law Record, Vol. 30, p. 490, RG 21, December 7, 1886-August 17, 1887, U.S. Court, Western District of Arkansas, Federal Archives and Records Center, Fort Worth, Texas.

[28]*Fort Smith Elevator*, July 22, 1887.

[29]Common Law Record, Vol. 30, RG 21, 1886 to August 17, 1887, U.S. Court, Western District of Arkansas, Federal Archives and Records Center, Fort Worth, Texas.

[30]Criminal Record, 1866-1896, Jacket #38, RG 21, U.S. Court, Western District of Arkansas, Federal Archives and Records Center, Fort Worth, Texas.

[31]*Ibid.*

[32]*Tahlequah Telephone*, July 20, 1887.

[33]Subpoena Record Book, 1887, p. 501, RG 21, U.S. Court, Western District of Arkansas, Federal Archives and Records Center, Fort Worth, Texas.

[34]*Ibid.*

[35]Interview of Robin Vann, by L.W. Wilson, November 12, 1937, Indian-Pioneer Papers, vol. 86, p. 472, Western History Collections, University of Oklahoma Library.

Chapter 7

[1]Interview of C.W. Costen, Indian-Pioneer Papers, vol. 21, p. 22, Western History Collections, University of Oklahoma Library.

[2]Interview of Roberta Hitchcock, Tahlequah, by Bonnie Speer, December 6, 1979.

[3]*Daily Oklahoman* (Oklahoma City), June 9, 1918.

[4]Interview of Roberta Hitchcock, Tahlequah, by Bonnie Speer, December 6, 1979.

[5]Interview of Robin Stann, by L.W. Wilson, November 12, 1937, Vol. 86, p. 472, Indian-Pioneer Papers, Western History Collections, University of Oklahoma Library.

[6]Interview of W.G.D. Hines, ADS 2-24-38, "Outlaw Ned Christie," Service Bureau of the South Research Department, FTP, Oklahoma, University of Wyoming, Laramie.

[7]*Ibid.*

[8]*Ibid.*

[9]Interview of Stanley A. Clark, by Jas. S. Buchanan, October 30, 1937, Vol. 18, pp. 206-215, Indian-Pioneer Papers, Western History Collections, University of Oklahoma Library.

[10]*Ibid.*

[11]*Ibid.*

[12]Interview of S.R. Lewis, Indian-Pioneer Papers, vol. 53, p. 438, Western History Collections, University of Oklahoma Library.

[13]Proceedings of the Executive Council, Cherokee Records, Vol. 71, p. 57, Indian History Collection, Oklahoma Historical Society.

[14]*Tahlequah Telephone*, August 19, 1887.

[15]*Fort Smith Elevator*, September 23, 1887.

[16]*Ibid.*

[17]Criminal Record, 1866-1896, John Parris, RG 21, Western District of Arkansas, Fort Smith, Federal Archives and Records Center, Fort Worth, Texas.

[18]*Fort Smith Elevator*, September 30, 1887.

[19]Criminal Record Jackets, 1866-1896, #E 57, Jacket #272, RG 21, Western District of Arkansas, Fort Smith, Federal Archives and Records Center, Fort Worth, Texas.

[20]*Ibid.*

[21]Colbert, Thomas Burnell, "Visionary Or Rogue? The Life & Legacy of Elias Cornelius," *Chronicles of Oklahoma*, Vol. No. 3, Fall, 1987, pp. 268-281.

[22]Wardell, Morris L., *A Political History of the Cherokee Nation*, University of Oklahoma Press, Norman, Oklahoma, 1938, p. 304.

Chapter 8

[1]*Tahlequah Advocate*, September 14, 1885.

[2]Interview of Lizzie Wilson Chair, Vol. 17, p. 18, Indian-Pioneer Papers, Western History Collections, University of Oklahoma Library.

[3]*Ibid.*, interview of Ransom Parris, Vol. 60, p. 478.

[4]*Ibid.*, interview of S.W. Ross, by Elizabeth Ross, Vol. 78, p. 249.

[5]Interview of Lucinda Wilhite by J.W. Tyner, Field Worker, Vol. 22, T-360-1, typescript, in the Doris Duke Indian Oral History Collection, Western History Collections, University of Oklahoma Library.

[6]Interview of William Wolfe, Vol. 12, p. 116, Indian-Pioneer Papers, Western History Collections, University of Oklahoma Library.

[7]*Ibid.*, interview of Alec Matheson, Vol. 61, p. 24.

[8]*Ibid.*, interview of G.F. Pedford by Carl B. Sherwood, December 15, 1937, Vol. 70, p. 187.

[9]*Ibid.*

[10]*Ibid.*

[11]Ballenger, T.L., *Around Tahlequah Council Fires*, Motter Bookbinding Co., Muskogee, Oklahoma, 1935, p. 72.

[12]Interview of John Christie, by Bonnie Speer, December 7, 1979.

[13]Interview of Alfred Seabolt, Vol. 81, p. 242, Indian-Pioneer Papers, Western History Collections, University of Oklahoma Library.

[14]Cherokee Nation Records, Cherokee Court Records, Court Transcript and Record of Hearing, pp. 255-56, Indian History Collection, Oklahoma Historical Society.

[15]*Ibid.*

[16]*Ibid.*

[17]*Ibid.*

[18]*Ibid.*

[19]Interview of Eli Wilson, by Wylie Thornton, July 26, 1937, Vol. 99, p. 142, Indian-Pioneer Papers, Western History Collections, University of Oklahoma Library.

Chapter 9

[1]Criminal Record, Jacket #272, E 57, RG 21, Western District of Arkansas, Fort Smith, Federal Archives and Records Center, Fort Worth, Texas.

[2]*Ibid.*

[3]*Fort Smith Elevator*, May 18, 1888.

[4]*Ibid.*, May 25, 1888.

[5]Criminal Record, Jacket #272, E 57, RG 21, Western District of Arkansas, Fort Smith, Federal Archives and Records Center, Fort Worth, Texas.

[6]*Indian Arrow* (Muskogee), October 18, 1888.

[7]Criminal Record, Jacket #272, E 57, RG 21, Western District of Arkansas, Fort Smith, Federal Archives and Records Center, Fort Worth, Texas.

[8]Shirley, Glenn, *The Law West of Fort Smith*, Henry Holt and Company, New York, New York, 1957, p. 59.

Chapter 10

[1]Interview of Beth Thomas Meeks by Bonnie Speer, February 27, 1979.

[2]*Fort Smith Elevator*, May 31, 1889.

[3]*Ibid.*, January 25, 1889.

[4]*Ibid.*, March 22, 1889.

[5]*Ibid.*, March 27, 1889.

[6]*Ibid.*, October 3, 1889.

[7]*Ibid.*

[8]Heck Thomas Day Book, 1889-90, owned by Beth Thomas Meeks, Norman, Oklahoma, p. 30.

[9]*Fort Smith Elevator*, October 3, 1889.

[10]Interview of Tuxie Miller by Annie R. Faulton, August 16, 1938, "Ned Christie, Cherokee Fugitive," Service Bureau of the Southwest Research Department, FTP, Oklahoma, University of Wyoming, Laramie.

[11] *Ibid.*

[12]*Fort Smith Elevator*, October 3, 1889.

[13]*Muskogee Phoenix*, October 3, 1889.

[14]*Fort Smith Elevator*, October 3, 1889.

[15]*Ibid.*

[16]*Ibid.*

[17]*Ibid.*

[18]*Muskogee Phoenix*, October 3, 1889.

Chapter 11

[1]Interview of John Henry Pedford by Carl B. Sherwood, December 15, 1937, Vol. 70, p. 187, Indian-Pioneer Papers, Western History Collections, University of Oklahoma Library.

[2]*Ibid.*, interview of Eli Wilson by Wylie Thornton, July 26, 1937, Vol. 99, p. 142.

[3]*Ibid.* Also see letter, Jacob Yoes, Department of Justice, to W.H.H. Miller, Attorney General, Washington, D. C., November 12, 1892, National Archives and Records Service, Washington, D.C.

[4]Interview of Eli Wilson by Wylie Thornton, July 26, 1937, Vol. 99, p. 142, Indian-Pioneer Papers, Western History Collections, University of Oklahoma Library.

[5]*Ibid.*, interview of Stanley A. Clark by Jas. S. Buchanan, October 30, 1937, Vol. 18, p. 208, Indian-Pioneer Papers, Western History Collections, University of Oklahoma Library.

[6]*Ibid.*

[7]*Fort Smith Elevator*, October 1, 1889.

[8]*Ibid.*, October 3, 1889.

[9]*Tahlequah Telephone*, October 3, 1889.

[10]*Ibid.*

[11]*Fort Smith Elevator*, October 1, 1889.

[12]Interview of Tuxie Miller by Annie R. Faulton, August 15, 1938, "Ned Christie, Cherokee Fugitive," Service Bureau of the Southwest Research Department, FTP, Oklahoma, University of Wyoming, Laramie.

[13]*Muskogee Phoenix*, October 3, 1889.

[14]*Ibid.*

[15]*Tahlequah Telephone*, October 3, 1889.

[16]*Ibid.*

[17]*Ibid.*

[18]*Ibid.*

[19]*Fort Smith Elevator*, October 11, 1890.

[20]*Ibid.*

[21]Interview of John Henry Pedford, by Carl B. Sherwood, December 15, 1937, Vol. 70, p. 187, Indian-Pioneer Papers, Western History Collections, University of Oklahoma Library.

[22]*Ibid.*

[23]*Daily Oklahoman* (Oklahoma City), June 9, 1918.

Chapter 12

[1]Interview of.T.L. Ballenger, Tahlequah, by Bonnie Speer, December 6, 1979.

[2]Interview of Robin Stann by L.W. Wilson, November 12, 1937, Vol. 86, p. 480, Indian-Pioneer Papers, Western History Collections, University of Oklahoma Library.

[3]*Ibid.*, interview with James R. Padgett, by Gus Hummingbird, May 13, 1937, S-149, Vol. 69, p. 15.

[4]*Ibid.*, interview with Elmira Stevens, by Wylie Thornton, February 4, 1938, Vol. 87, p. 278.

[5]*Fort Smith Elevator*, November 11, 1889.

[6]Heck Thomas Day Book, 1889-1890, owned by Beth Thomas Meeks, Norman, Oklahoma, p. 32.

[7]*Ibid.*

[8]Steele, Phillip, *The Last Cherokee Warriors*, Pelican Publishing Company, Gretna, Louisiana, 1974, p. 91.

[9]Heck Thomas Day Book, 1889-1890, owned by Beth Thomas Meeks, p. 41.

[10]Meeks, Beth Thomas with Bonnie Speer, *Heck Thomas, My Papa*, Levite of Apache, Norman, 1988, p. 19.

[11]Heck Thomas Day Book, 1889-1890, owned by Beth Thomas Meeks, p. 41.

[12]Shirley, Glenn, *Belle Starr and Her Times*, University of Oklahoma Press, Norman, 1982, p. 218.

[13]*Ibid*

[14]*Ibid.*

[15]Ibid.

[16]*Fort Smith Elevator*, January 24, 1890.

[17]*Ibid.*, January 31, 1890.

[18]*Ibid.*, January 24, 1890.

[19]*Ibid.*, January 31, 1890.

[20]Baker, Elmer LeRoy, *Gunman's Territory*, The Naylor Company, San Antonio, Texas, 1969, p. 135.

[21]*Tahlequah Telephone*, February 9, 1890.

[22]Interview of Eli Wilson by Wylie Thornton, July 26, 1937, Vol. 99, p. 142, Indian-Pioneer Papers, Western History Collections, University of Oklahoma Library.

[23]*Ibid.*, interview of John Henry Pedford by Carl B. Sherwood, December 15, 1937, Vol. 70, p. 187.

[24]*Fort Smith Elevator*, November 7, 1890.

[25] Interview of James R. Padgett by Gus Hummingbird, May 13, 1937, S-149, Vol. 69, p. 15, Indian-Pioneer Papers, Western History Collections, University of Oklahoma Library.

[26]*Ibid.*, interview of Stanley A. Clark by Jas. S. Buchanan, October 30, 1937, Vol. 18, p. 207.

Chapter 13

[1]Report, RG 60, Department of Justice from W.E. Hazen, Examiner, Subject: "report [sic] Ref. Examination ofice [sic] and ofcs. [sic] of Jacob Yoes, U.S. Mar., Wn. Ark.," March 1890, National Archives and Records Service, Washington, D.C.

[2]Cherokee Nation, Roll of the Cherokee Census, 1890, Oklahoma Historical Society.

[3]*Ibid.*, Cherokee Census Roll, 1900, p. 498.

[4]*Ibid.*, 1902, #733.

[5]Patients Register, Case File 9653, Arch Wolf, Synopsis of Record, Record Group No. 418, National Archives and Records Service, Washington, D.C.

[6]*Arkansas Gazette*, November 8, 1892.

[7]Interview of Lucinda Sanders Wilhite by J.W. Tyner, Field Worker, December 23, 1968, Vol. 22, T-360-1, typescript in the Doris Duke Indian Oral History Collection, Western History Collections, University of Oklahoma Library.

[8]*Ibid.*

[9]*Ibid.*, interview of Catherine Wilhite, by B.D. Timmons, August 18, 1967, Vol. 22, T-135, p. 7, Doris Duke Indian Oral History Collection in the Western History Collections, University of Oklahoma Library.

[10]Interview of T.L. Ballenger by Bonnie Speer, December 6, 1979.

[11]Criminal Record, RG 21, Western District of Arkansas, Fort Smith, Federal Archives and Records Center, Fort Worth, Texas.

[12]Interview of T.L. Ballenger by Bonnie Speer, December 6, 1979.

[13]*Fort Smith Elevator*, October 31, 1980.

[14]*Ibid.*, November 7, 1890.

[15]Court Orders, RG 21, Federal Archives and Records Center, Fort Worth, Texas.

Chapter 14

[1]Interview of Robin Stann by L.W. Wilson, November 12, 1937, Vol. 86, p. 480, Indian-Pioneer Papers, Western History Collections, University of Oklahoma Library.

[2]Interview of Allene J. Davis by Bonnie Speer, December 7, 1979.

[3]Interview of Eli Wilson by Wylie Thornton, July 26, 1937, Vol. 142, p. 99, Indian-Pioneer Papers, Western History Collections, University of Oklahoma Library.

[4]*Ibid.*

[5]*Fort Smith Elevator*, August 1, 1890.

[6]*Ibid.*, June 13, 1889.

[7]Interview of William Hugh Winder, by Wylie Thornton, November 5, 1937, Vol. 99, p. 293, Indian-Pioneer Papers, Western History Collections, University of Oklahoma Library.

[8]McKennon, C.H., *Iron Men*, Doubleday and Company, Inc., Garden City, New York, 1967, p. 99.

[9]*Ibid.*, p. 98.

[10]*Ibid.*

[11]*Ibid.*

[12]Shirley, Glenn, *The Law West of Fort Smith*, Henry Holt & Company, New York, New York, 1957, p. 48.

[13]McKennon, C. H., *Iron Men*, Doubleday and Company, Inc., Garden City, New York, p. 98.

Chapter 15

[1]Criminal Record, RG 21, Western District of Arkansas, Fort Smith, Federal Archives and Records Center, Fort Worth, Texas.

[2]*Ibid.*

[3]*Ibid.*, #E57, Jacket 286, February 1893.

[4]*Ibid.*

[5]McKennon, C.H., *Iron Men*, Doubleday and Company, Inc., Garden City, New York, 1967, p. 135.

[6]Criminal Records, RG 21, Box 231, Jacket #348, Western District of Arkansas, Fort Smith, Federal Archives and Records Center, Fort Worth, Texas.

[7]*Evening Gazette* (Oklahoma City), October 13, 1892.

[8]*Ibid.*, Criminal Records, RG 21, Box 231, Jacket #348.

[9]Interview of John Mountz, Vol. 65, p. 325, Indian-Pioneer Papers, Western History Collections, University of Oklahoma Library.

[10]*Evening Gazette* (Oklahoma City), October 13, 1892.

[11]*Ibid.*

[12]*Ibid.*

[13]*Ibid.*

[14]*Fort Smith Elevator*, December 30, 1892.

[15]Criminal Records, Record Group 21, Jacket #479, Western District of Arkansas, Fort Smith, Federal Archives and Records Center, Fort Worth, Texas.

[16]*Evening Gazette* (Oklahoma City), November 7, 1892.

[17]Letter, Jacob Yoes to W.H.H. Miller, Attorney-General, U.S., Washington, D.C., November 12, 1892, RG 60, Western District of Arkansas, Fort Smith, National Archives and Records Service, Washington, D.C.

[18]Starr, Henry, *Thrilling Events, Life of Henry Starr, Written In the Colorado Penitentiary By Himself* , July 1914, p. 38.

[19]*Ibid.*, p. 74

[20]McKennon, C.H., *Iron Men*, Doubleday and Company, Inc., Garden City, New York, 1967, p. 119.

[21]Interview of Stanley A. Clark, by Jas. S. Buchanan, October 30, 1937, vol. 18, p. 207, Indian-Pioneer Papers, Western History Collections, University of Oklahoma Library.

[22]McKennon, C.J., *Iron Men*, Doubleday and Company, Inc., Garden City, New York, p. 119.

[23]Interview of Roberta Hitchcock by Bonnie Speer, December 6, 1979.

[24]McKennon, C.J., *Iron Men*, Doubleday and Company, Inc., Garden City, New York, 1967, p. 129.

[25]*Ibid.*, p. 133.

[26]*Ibid.*, p. 134.

[27]*Ibid.*, p. 130.

[28]*Ibid* ., p. 129

[29]*Tulsa World*, October 5, 1952.

[30]*Arkansas Gazette* (Little Rock), November 8, 1892.

[31]McKennon, C. J., *Iron Men*, Doubleday and Company, Inc., Garden City, New York, p. 136.

[32]*Arkansas Gazette* (Little Rock), November 8, 1892.

[33]*Muskogee Phoenix*, November 10, 1892.

Chapter 16

[1]*Arkansas Gazette* (Little Rock), November 8, 1892.

[2]Interview of W. L. "Tuxie" Miller, Muskogee, Oklahoma, GH/8-16-38, Service Bureau of the South, Research Department, FTP Oklahoma, University of Wyoming, Laramie.

[3]*Arkansas Gazette* (Little Rock), November 8, 1892.

[4]*Muskogee Phoenix*, November 10, 1892.

[5]*Evening Gazette* (Oklahoma City), November 7, 1892.

[6]*Arkansas Gazette* (Little Rock), November 8, 1892.

[7]*Muskogee Phoenix*, November 10, 1892.

[8]*Arkansas Gazette* (Little Rock), November 8, 1892.

[9]Interview of Tuxie Miller by L.W. Wilson, March 15-17, 1937, Vol. 63, p. 284, Indian-Pioneer Papers, Western History Collections, University of Oklahoma Library.

[10]*Evening Gazette* (Oklahoma City), November 7, 1892.

[11]*Muskogee Phoenix*, November 10, 1892.

[12]*Evening Gazette* (Oklahoma City), November 7, 1892.

[13]Interview of Wiley Wolf, by J.W. Tyner, Field Worker, January 10, 1969, Vol. 22, T-370, typescript, Doris Duke Collection, Western History Collection, University of Oklahoma Library.

[14]*Ibid.*

[15]Interview of Stanley A. Clark, by Jas. S. Buchanan, October 30, 1937, Vol. 18, p. 207, Indian-Pioneer Papers, Western History Collections, University of Oklahoma Library.

[16]*Arkansas Gazette* (Little Rock), November 8, 1892.

[17]McKennon, C.H., *Iron Men*, Doubleday and Company, Inc., Garden City, New York, 1967, p. 148.

[18]*Arkansas Gazette* (Little Rock), November 8, 1892.

[19]Interview of Jeff Tindel by J.W. Tyner, Field Worker, January 10, 1969, Vol. 22, T-554-1, typescript Doris Duke Collection, Western History Collections, University of Oklahoma Library.

[20]*Arkansas Gazette* (Little Rock), November 8, 1892.

[21]*Tulsa World*, October 5,1952.

[22]*Evening Gazette* (Oklahoma City), November 7, 1892.

[23]*Ibid.*

[24]*Tulsa World*, October 5, 1952.

[25]*Muskogee Phoenix*, November 10, 1892.

[26]*Arkansas Gazette* (Little Rock), November 8, 1892.

[27]*Muskogee Phoenix*, November 10, 1892.

[28]*Arkansas Gazette* (Little Rock), November 8, 1892.

[29]*Tulsa World*, October 5, 1952.

[30]*Arkansas Gazette* (Little Rock), November 8, 1892.

[31]*Ibid.*

[32]Letter, Jacob Yoes to W.H.H. Miller, Attorney-General, U.S., Washington, D.C., November 12, 1892, RG 60, Western District of Arkansas, Fort Smith, National Archives and Record Service, Washington, D.C.

[33]Interview of Wiley Wolf, by J. W. Tyner, Field Worker, January 10, 1969, V. 22, T-370-2, in The Doris Duke Indian Oral History Collection, Western History Collections, University of Oklahoma Library.

[34]*Muskogee Phoenix*, November 10, 1892.

[35]Interview of Stanley A. Clark, by Jas. S. Buchanan, October 30, 1937, Vol. 18, p. 207, Indian-Pioneer Papers, Western History Collections, University of Oklahoma Library.

[36]*Tulsa World*, October 5, 1952.

[37]Interview of Stanley A. Clark, by Jas. S. Buchanan, October 30, 1937, Vol. 18, p. 207, Indian-Pioneer Papers, Western History Collections, University of Oklahoma Library.

[38]*Tulsa World*, October 5, 1952.

[39]Letter, Mrs. Bettie Halsell, Fayetteville, Arkansas, to Bonnie Speer, March 17, 1980.

[40]Interview of Jefferson Tindall by J.W. Tyner, Feb. 9, 1970, Vol. 20, T-554-1, typescript, in The Doris Duke Indian Oral History Collection, Western History Collections, University of Oklahoma Library.

[41]File, C.B. Rhodes, Photographic Archives, Western History Collections, University of Oklahoma.

Chapter 17

[1]*Evening Gazette*, (Oklahoma City) November 7, 1892.

[2]*Muskogee Phoenix*, November 10, 1892.

[3]*Arkansas Gazette* (Little Rock), November 8, 1892.

[4]*Muskogee Phoenix*, November 10, 1892.

[5]Interview of Roberta Hitchcock, Tahlequah, by Bonnie Speer, December 6, 1979.

[6]*Evening Gazette* (Oklahoma City), November 7, 1892.

[7]File, Ned Christie, typescript, Cherokee Room, Northeastern State University, Tahlequah, Oklahoma. Also, original in possession of Mrs. Allene J. Davis.

[8]*Muskogee Phoenix*, November 10, 1892.

[9]*Fort Smith Call* as reprinted in the *Muskogee Phoenix*, November 10, 1892.

[10]Steele, Phillip, *The Last Cherokee Warriors*, Pelican Publishing Company, Gretna, Louisiana, 1974.

[11]*Muskogee Phoenix*, November 10, 1892.

[12]Interview of Allene J. Davis by Bonnie Speer, May 7, 1980.

[13]*Arkansas Gazette*, (Little Rock) November 5, 1892.

[14]*Fort Smith Elevator*, December 30, 1892.

[15]*Daily Oklahoman* (Oklahoma City), June 9, 1918.

[16]*Vinita Leader* (Cherokee Nation), January 9, 1896.

[17]Interview of W.L. "Tuxie" Miller, Muskogee, Oklahoma, GH/8-16-38, Service Bureau of the South, Research Department, FTP, Oklahoma, University of Wyoming.

[18]Criminal Records, Jacket #479, RG 21, Western District of Arkansas, Fort Smith, Federal Archives and Records Center, Fort Worth, Texas.

[19]Sentence Record Books, 1884-1909, Box IX, #81-5-7, Penitentiary 6-10-1891 to 10-12-1894, p. 301, RG 21, Western District of Arkansas, Fort Smith, Federal Archives and Records Service, Fort Worth, Texas.

[20]Steele, Phillip, *The Last Cherokee Warriors*, Pelican Publishing Company, Gretna, Louisiana, 1974 p. 104.

[21]Criminal Record, Jacket #479, p. 491, RG 21, Western District of Arkansas, Fort Smith, Federal Archives and Records Service, Fort Worth, Texas.

[22]Patients Register, Case File 9653, Arch Wolf, RG 418.

[23]*Ibid.*, undated letter, to W.W. Godding, M.D., from Arch Christie, Record Group 418, Washington, D.C.

[24] *Ibid.*, Patients Register, Case File 9653, Arch Wolf, RG 418.

[25]Letter, Mrs. Bettie Halsell, Fayetteville, Arkansas, to Bonnie Speer, March 17, 1980.

[26]*Watonga Republican*, July 12, 1893.

[27]Interview of Jefferson Tindall, by J.W. Tyner, Field Worker, February 9, 1970, Vol. 20, T-554-1, typescript Doris Duke Collection, Western History Collections, University of Oklahoma Library.

[28]Interview of Edward Hines, by W.J. Bigby, August 16, 1937, Vol. 65, p. 325, Indian-Pioneer Papers, Western History Collections, University of Oklahoma Library.

Appendix

[1]Letter, Jacob Yoes to W.H.H. Miller, Attorney-General, Washington, D.C., December 12, 1892, RG 21, Western District of Arkansas, Fort Smith, National Archives and Records Service, Washington, D.C.

BIBLIOGRAPHY

INTERVIEWS

Ballenger, T.L., Tahlequah, December 6, 1979.

Christie, John and Rachel, Stillwell, December 7, 1979.

Davis Allene J., Stillwell, May 6-7, 1980.

Hitchcock, Mrs. Roberta, December 6, 1979; May 7, 1980.

Jones, Mrs. Beatrice Maples, phone, February 11, 1980.

Long, Mrs. Ruth, December 6, 1979; May 6-8, 1980.

Meeks, Mrs. Beth Thomas, February 27, 1979.

Teague, Roberta, May 7, 1980.

LETTERS

Ballenger, T.L., Tahlequah, Oklahoma, to Bonnie Speer, Norman, Oklahoma, January 25, 1980; May 15, 1980; May 23, 1980.

Barnes & Mellette, Attorneys at Law, Fort Smith, Arkansas, to Dr. W.M. Godding, Washington, D.C., March 9, 1986. Washington, D.C., RG 418, Western District of Arkansas, National Archives and Records Service, Washington, D.C.

Christie, Arch, Wauhillau, Indian Territory, to W.W. Godding, M.D., Washington, D.C., undated, Washington, D.C., RG 418, Western District of Arkansas, Federal Archives and Records Service Washington, D.C.

Christie, Arch, Wauhillau, Indian Territory, to Dr. C.H. Latimer, Washington, D.C., October 19, 1895, RG 418, Western District of Arkansas, Federal Archives and Records Service, Washington, D.C.

Christie, Mrs. John, Stillwell, Oklahoma, to Bonnie Speer, Norman, Oklahoma, January 23, 1980; July 16, 1980.

Churchill, James A., esq., Clerk of the U.S. District Court, Fort Smith, from Judge, U.S. District Court, Little

Rock, July 9, 1984, Western History Collections, University of Oklahoma, "Letters to James 0. Churchill."

Crowson, Thomas J., Fort Smith Historic Site, Fort Smith, Arkansas, to Bonnie Speer, Norman, Oklahoma, January 3, 1980.

Davis, Allene J., Stillwell, Oklahoma, to Bonnie Speer, Norman, Oklahoma, March 1, 1980; June 1, 1980; July 10, 1980, July 10, 1980.

Halsell, Mrs. Bettie, Fayetteville, Arkansas, to Bonnie Speer, Norman, Oklahoma, March 17, 1980.

Hitchcock, Mrs. Roberta, Tahlequah, Oklahoma, to Bonnie Speer, Norman, Oklahoma, November 11, 1979; September 4, 1980; September 4, 1980.

Hagerstrand, M.A., Executive Vice President, The Cherokee National Historical Society, Inc., Tahlequah, Oklahoma, Tsa-La-Gi, to Bonnie Speer, Norman, Oklahoma, February 18, 1980; January 18, 1980; December 17, 1979.

Lester, A.D., Westville, Oklahoma, to Bonnie Speer, Norman, Oklahoma, February 1, 1980; February 9, 1980.

Steele, Phillip, Springdale, Arkansas, to Bonnie Speer, Norman, Oklahoma, November 20, 1979; January 28, 1980; April 15, 1980; April 23, 1980; January 10, 1980; February 6, 1980.

Teague, Roberta, Stillwell, Oklahoma, to Bonnie Speer, Norman, Oklahoma, January 9, 1980; February 10, 1980.

Vick, Ginsie, Tahlequah, Oklahoma, to Bonnie Speer, Norman, Oklahoma, September 17, 1980.

Young,Chas. E., Wauhillau, Indian Territory, to W.W. Godding, Washington, D.C., January 6, 1896; July 6, 1896; February 3, 1898, January 2, 1900, Case File 9653, Arch Wolf, RG 418, National Archives and Records Service, Washington, D.C.,

Young, Chas. E., Wauhillau, Indian Territory, to A.B. Richardson, M.D., Washington, D.C., January 1, 1900, Washington, D.C., Case File 9653, Arch Wolf, RG 418, National Archives and Records Service, Washington, D.C.

Census Records, Cherokee Rolls, 1890, Freedmen.

Census Roll of Cherokees East of Mississippi, 1835.

Cherokee Census Rolls, Cherokee Nation, 1835, 1880, 1890 by blood, 1892, 1896, 1906.

Cherokee Emigration Rolls 1817-1835, Muster Roll.

Cherokee Evaluations, North Carolina, 1836, Welch & Garrett, No. 14, National Archives, Record Group 75, E 236, Miscelleanous Claims, Washington, D.C.

Cherokee Court Records, pp. 255-56, Court Transcript and Record of Hearing, Cherokee Nation Records, Oklahoma Historical Society, Oklahoma City, Oklahoma.

Common Law Record, Vol. 31, U.S. District Court, Western District of Arkansas, Record Group 21, Federal Archives and Records Center, Fort Worth, Texas.

Common Record, Vol. 31, November Term 1887, pp. 366 & 441, Cherokee Nation Records, Oklahoma Historical Society.

Court Criminal Cases, p. 95, "Cherokee Nation vs. Ned Christie for Murder," Cherokee Nation Records, Oklahoma Historical Society.

Criminal Record, Jackets 1866-1896, RG 21, U.S. Court, Western District of Arkansas, Federal Archives and Records Center, Fort Worth, Texas.

Final Rolls of the Cherokees, Dawes Commission, 1902.

Henderson Roll of Eastern Cherokees 1835 and Index.

Mullay Roll of North Carolina Cherokees, 1848.

Patients Register, Case File 9653, Arch Wolf, RG 418, Western District of Arkansas, National Archives and Records Center, Washington, D.C.

Proceedings of the Executive Council, Cherokee Nation, 1885-1887, Vol. 710, Cherokee Nation Records, Indian History Collection, Oklahoma Historical Society.

Proceedings of the National Council, Cherokee Nation, Extra Session, April 12, 1886, p. 107; Regular Session, 1885-1887; Special Session, May 1887, p. 208, Indian History Collection, Oklahoma Historical Society.

"Report Ref. Examination ofice [sic] and ofcs. [sic] of Jacob Yoes, U.S. Mar. Wn. Ark." March 28, 1890, W. E. Hazen to the Department of Justice, Record Group 60, National Archives and Records Service, Washington, D.C.

Roster, First Cherokee Mounted Rifles, Cherokee Nation Records, Oklahoma Historical Society, Oklahoma City, Oklahoma.

Sentence Record Book, RG 21, Western District of Arkansas, Federal Archives and Records Center, Fort Worth, Texas.

Subpoena Record Book, 1887, p. 501, RG 21, Western District of Arkansas, Federal Archives and Records Center, Fort Worth, Texas.

COLLECTIONS

Christie, Ned, Folder, Cherokee Room, Northeastern State University, Tahlequah, Oklahoma, including typescript, "Affidavit of Death," and typescript, "Life of Ned Christie," by Mildred Wright.

Doris Duke Collection, Western History Collections, University of Oklahoma, numerous interviews.

Draper Collection, Vol. IXX, p. 58, January 28, 1783, University of Oklahoma, Western History Collections, University of Oklahoma Library.

Indian-Pioneer Papers, Western History Collections, University of Oklahoma, numerous interviews, 1937-1938.

Outlaws, The National Archives, record Group 69, WPA/FTP, Oklahoma Research, "Ned Christie, Cherokee Fugitive," interview with Tuxie Miller, by Annie R. Faulton, August 16, 1938; "Outlaw, Ned Christie," source Ned P. Dewitt in *Oklahoma News*, March 14, 1937; "Outlaw, Ned Christie," source, *Tulsa Democrat*, June 15, 1938; interview with W.G.D.Hines, December 19, 1938.

Thomas Papers, private papers of Deputy Marshal Heck Thomas, in possession of Mrs. Beth Thomas Meeks, Norman, Oklahoma.

Tsa-La-Gi, Oral History Museum, Historical Soociety of the Cherokee Nation, Tahlequah, Oklahoma.

Western History Collections, University of Oklahoma, E.C. Boudinot Papers, Box 48, #11.

NEWSPAPERS

Arkansas Gazette (Little Rock), October to November, 1892.

Bentonville ____, (Arkansas), May ____, 1887.

The Cherokee Advocate (Tahlequah) 1885 to 1895.

Daily Oklahoman (Oklahoma City), June 9, 1918; "The Tragedy of Going Snake Court House," Grant Foreman, October 7, 1954; February 10, 1957.

Fayetteville Democrat (Arkansas), May 13, 1887.

Fort Smith Democrat, 1885 to 1895.

Globe Democrat (Fort Smith), October 23, 1887.

Indian Arrow (Muskogee), October 18, 1888.

Muskogee Indian Journal 1885 to 1895.

Muskogee Phoenix, 1885 to 1895.

Siloam Springs Herald (Arkansas), May 13, 1887.

Tahlequah Telephone, June 1887 to 1895.

Tulsa World "91 Gunfight With Outlaw Still Vivid," by Gilbert Asher, interview with Wess Bowman, October 5, 1952.

Tulsa Democrat, August 18, 1918.

Indian Chieftain, (Vinita, Cherokee Nation), 1887 to 1895.

Vinita Leader January 9, 1896.

PERIODICALS

Chronicles of Oklahoma, Summer 1985, "A Legacy of Education: The History of the Cherokee Seminaries," by Brad Agnew.

Chronicles of Oklahoma, Vol. 63, No. 3, Fall 1987, "Visionary Or Rogue? The Life & Legacy of Elias Cornelius Boudinot," by Thomas Burnell Colbert.

Chronicles of Oklahoma, Vol. 18, p. 101, "Mrs. Anna C. Trainor Matheson," by herself.

Orbit Magazine, February 27, 1977, "The Man Who Killed Ned Christie," by Aileen Stroud Libke.

Strum's Oklahoma Magazine, Vol. 11, September 1910, No. 1, p. 25.

PAMPHLET

"Fort Smith," Government Printing Office, 1972.

UNPUBLISHED

"Cherokee National Capitol Building, 1867-1979," Cherokee Historical Society, Tahlequah, Oklahoma.

"Historic American Buildings, Survey," Cherokee National Capitol Building, Cherokee Historical Society, Tahlequah, Oklahoma.

"Records from the Historic American Buildings Survey," compiled by Historic American Buildings Survey Office of Archeology and Historic Preservation, National Park Service.

"Fort Gibson Stockade," National Park Service, leaflet.

BOOKS

The American Ephemeris & Nautical Almanac, for the year 1887, Washington: Bureau of Navigation, 1889, p. 85.

Baker, Elmer LeRoy, *Gunman's Territory*, The Naylor Company, San Antonio, Texas, 1969.

Ballenger, T.L. *Around Tahlequah Council Fires*, Motter Bookbinding Co., Muskogee, Oklahoma, 1935.

Breihan, Carl W., with Charles A. Rosamond, *The Bandit Belle*, Hangman Press, Superior Publishing Company, Seattle, Washington, 1970.

Bruchac, Joseph, ed., *Songs From This Earth On Turtle's Back,* Greenfield Review Press, New York, New York, 1983.

Conley, Robert J., *Back To Malachi*, Doubleday and Company, Inc., Garden City, New York, New York, 1986.

Foreman, Carolyn Thomas, *Park Hill*, The Press of the Star Printery, Inc., Muskogee, Oklahoma, 1948.

Harman, S.W., *Hell On the Border; He Hanged Eighty-Eight Men*, compiled by C.P. Sterns, The Phoenix Publishing Company, Fort Smith, Arkansas, 1898.

Harman, Samuel W., *Hell On the Border*, Hell On the Border Publishing Co., Fort Smith, Arkansas, 1953, copyright Frank L. Van Eaton.

Harman, Samuel W., *Hell On the Border*, Edited by Jack Gregory and Rennard Strickland, Indian Heritage Association, Muskogee, Oklahoma, 1971.

McKennon, C.H., *Iron Men*, Doubleday and Co., Inc., Garden City, New York, 1967.

Oskison, John, *Black Jack Davy*, D. Appleton and Company, New York-London, 1926.

Shirley, Glenn, *Belle Starr and Her Times*, University of Oklahoma Press, Norman, Oklahoma, 1983.

Shirley, Glenn, *Last of the Badmen*, David McKay Co., Inc., New York, New York, 1965.

Shirley, Glenn, *Law West of Fort Smith*, Henry Holt and Co., New York, New York, 1957.

Starr, Emmett, *History of the Cherokees*, The Warden Co., Oklahoma City, Oklahoma, 1921.

Starr, Henry, *Thrilling Events, Life of Henry Starr, Written in the Colorado Penitentiary By Himself*, published July, 1914, and sold by R. D. Gordon, Tulsa, Oklahoma.

Steele, Phillip, *The Last Cherokee Warriors*, Pelican Publishing Company, Gretna, Louisiana, 1974.

Thoburn, Joseph H., *History of Oklahoma*, Vol. III, The American Historical Society, Chicago & New York, 1916.

Tyner, James W. and Alice Tyner Simmons, *Our People and Where They Rest*, Volumes 1 to 10, American Indian Institute, University of Oklahoma, Norman, Oklahoma, 1973.

Wardell, Morris, L., *A Political History of the Cherokee Nation*, University of Oklahoma Press, Norman, Oklahoma, 1938.

Watts, J.W., *Cherokee Citizenship and A Brief History of Internal Affairs in the Cherokee Nation With Records and Acts of the National Council From 1871 To Date*, Register Print, Muldrow, Indian Territory, 1895.

Woodward, Grace Steele, *The Cherokees*, University of Oklahoma Press, Norman, Oklahoma, 1963.

INDEX

169

More than one hundred years have passed since Ned Christie w shot by deputies in his log fort east of Tahlequah. A form Cherokee legislator, he was accused of killing a U.S. Depu Marshal. He refused to give himself up and stand trial for fear he wou not receive a fair trial in Issac "Hanging Judge" Parker's court in Fc Smith, Arkansas. Soon he became known as one of the most notorio outlaws in Indian Territory. Finally he was blasted out of his home wi dynamite and killed. Was he guilty of the crimes of which he w accused? Today, the legends of his exploits still ring in the Cherokee hi he called home.

"The Killing of Ned Christie is the most carefully researched and best doc mented book ever written on an Indian Territory 'outlaw.' Bonnie Speer 's infc mative presentation of the story allows the reader to judge for himself if Chris. was an outlaw."

-**Dee Cordury**, founder and president of Oklahombr

"A good book."

-**Larry McMurtry**, author, *Zeke and N.*

"He was a very clever man. If he had been a soldier he would have been one the greatest of generals. Ned Christie was one of the bravest in the South West
-**Edward Hines**, Christie contempora

Bonnie Speer has spent many years publishing nonfiction. She graduated from the University of Oklahoma in 1976 with an M.A. in professional writing, journalism department. Author of eleven published books and over three hundred articles, she is an adjunct professor of journalism, University of Oklahoma. She is a member of Oklahoma Writers' Federation, Oklahombres, and Women Writing the West.

90000

ISBN 1-889683-13-2

9 781889 683133